Bound *by* Belief

Bound *by* Belief

SHIVI SETHI

Srishti
Publishers & Distributors

Srishti Publishers & Distributors
A unit of AJR Publishing LLP
212A, Peacock Lane
Shahpur Jat, New Delhi – 110 049

editorial@srishtipublishers.com

First Published by Srishti Publishers & Distributors in 2025

10 9 8 7 6 5 4 3 2 1

For my Vyom & Maitrey –
May your inner light forever outshine every doubt
the world dares to place before you.

Chapter 1

She found me when I thought I'd be lost forever. She caressed my cheek, and it felt as though I'd finally found home. I am a book, yes. But I could feel my heart finding its rhythm with each word she read, and every touch she offered me. It wasn't that I'd never been touched before or that I'd never been read. I had met those who cherished me and held me close when I was overwhelmed. But she was different. Her mere glance was enough to make me want to go with her and stay by her side forever, or for as long as she wished.

Centuries old, I am. The wear and tear of time has taken its toll, and I only hoped no one would tell her so. I didn't want her to think I was unworthy, to hesitate, or doubt whether I was worth taking home. Oh, how I wished in that moment that I could be worthy of her attention!

The moment we were seen together, I could sense the disapproval from others. They tried to change her mind, tried to talk her out of choosing something so 'worthless' in their eyes. The yellowed pages and torn edges made me appear unworthy, I suppose. But not to her. She was relentless. She was the fire I would gladly let consume me.

And so, there I was... Won over and claimed, ending up beside her. She held me close to her heart, and I could feel her happiness, her relief at having found me. How rare it is, how surreal, to finally meet the one you've been written for.

I was known as the *Book of the Unknown*, filled with verses from various languages and cultures, a mystery only a few dared to unravel. Curiosity kept me intact over generations. But why was I here now, in a dusty antique store, sold as a vintage collectable at the cost of mere pennies… That, my friends, is destiny's design.

You are where you are meant to be, if only you can surrender to life's lessons. We each walk a journey meant for us. Life trains and teaches us lessons designed to foster the greatness we seek. So when the right moment arrives, we must believe we are precisely where we need to be. Every obstacle, every crossroad we tread, is in reality a testing and training ground, taking us a step closer to our dreams.

My journey began in the early '70s when someone decided to translate a mythical story about a magical world into a more common language. Not many copies were made, but I was among the first: a prized possession, the original. Nobody knew who my author was, but it seemed like my translator had insight. Nevertheless, it still took years before I was translated into a readable story.

In my early days, like everyone else, the desire to find my life's purpose kept me on my toes. Every time a reader held me close and tried to read my thoughts, I would wait to return to my original self and be appreciated for what I was, what I am capable of. But I guess it was not for common eyes to see and acknowledge what I truly held.

Over the years, I learned that I was meant to be difficult to decipher. Not everyone can read between the lines. I was made difficult to understand on purpose. My words were meant to reveal their secrets only to the one destined to uncover them. Thus, for everyone else, I remained a mystery. A story, nevertheless, but one that hinted at greatness in the right pair of hands.

And so, as a unique, odd manuscript, I spent years in isolation. Loneliness no longer pained me; isolation had become my companion. But here, with her, I felt seen for the first time.

Seeing her enter the world of the unknown and wanting to decipher my story... her story... it was a sight I would always hold close to my heart. My heart, like every other book lying at the core, the book's spine, warmed at her touch. That's exactly when the first change happened.

A simple girl as she was, she didn't realize it at first, but for the first time in centuries, my title became visible. I was no longer a nameless relic. My real name, the one my creator had given me, inked itself onto my heart, visible for the world to see.

I learned her name when she signed herself onto the front register, marking the fact that I now belonged to her. Rose, she wrote with the boldest "*R*."

Rose was beautiful, with a childlike smile, and ladylike features. Her long, wavy brown hair cascaded over her shoulders down to her waist. Tiny twirls framed her ears. She captivated my heart simply with the way she looked around the store—the awe in her eyes as they wandered through the antique shop, yet the quiet contentment of her find resting in her arms.

Her olive-green eyes held hints of brown, as though nature itself had marked her as part of its own. And her smile... she smiled her way into my heart, melting the layers of weariness I had carried for centuries, all becoming a part of the past.

Little did I know, this love was destined to consume me. But even such knowledge wouldn't have changed a thing. I was ready to turn myself to ashes if that's what it took to introduce her to her real self.

Thanking the storekeeper and holding me close, Rose stepped onto the street, and I proudly changed my colour from russet to deep emerald green.

She was magic to me, and magic was what I was meant to ignite in her.

The moment we stepped out of that antique store, I was no longer a relic. Though I was born centuries ago, it felt like I had only now come alive. My heart glowed with warmth, my veins pulsed with energy, and the roots of the ancient tree enveloped the edges of my form. My physical body transformed the very night when her story and mine began.

As we walked, I noticed a sadness in her gaze. The closer we got to her home, the dimmer her smile became, as if a heavy thought weighed on her heart. It was one of those moments when, though you've just met someone, all you want to do is lend them your shoulder. To let them know that, no matter how hard it might be to believe, they will never be alone again, that the words may fall short, but the belief you have in them never will.

Her eyes fell on me, as if, somehow, she heard me without my trying.

Rose turned the book's front cover towards her and hugged me, as though she knew I was beaming with the warmth of having found both my love and my life's purpose, and vice versa.

Rose lived alone, as I had guessed. As soon as we reached her home, she set me aside and went to freshen up, or so I presumed. With my years of experience with readers, I knew I wouldn't be opened on the very first day, so I kept my patience.

She placed me carefully on her bedside table, then, with a sigh, turned to finish her tasks for the day. She changed into a sky-blue T-shirt and black shorts, tying her hair in a loose ponytail. Even without trying, she was a delightful sight, her simplicity radiating a quiet beauty. No one would have guessed that this seemingly innocent, petite woman held within her an epitome of power, waiting to be awakened.

In the days that followed, I came to understand her life better. Rose worked for a local magazine, writing pieces that didn't seem to excite her. Her work was methodical, lacking the spark I'd seen in her eyes when she first held me. Yet, at the end of each day, I would sense her relief. Every night, after closing her computer, she would reach for a notebook adorned with a night-sky print, jotting down words that finally brought a smile to her face.

Then, on the seventh night, she finally picked me up again. Holding me close to her heart, she whispered that she'd been waiting for this moment and was happy to finally have the time to read me.

Now that I was in her hands, I could feel myself transforming. To be true to one's nature, what joy it is! Finding someone who is not only glad to have found you but also lets you be yourself without judgment. Everything feels like magic with them. When Rose first saw me in the bookstore, she only saw fragments of who I was. Nevertheless, she trusted her heart's inclination to take me home and try to understand me better. That little step of not only acknowledging the other person as different but also granting oneself the chance to understand them better… at the very least, I could allow this relationship to be based on the ultimate truth about myself and let her see my whole self.

As she ran her fingers along my spine, spirals of energy seemed to pass through me. The story hidden in my pages began making its way through the lines meant for common eyes and was ready to reveal itself to her. Surprisingly, the words coming forth from between the lines were woven in a language that only she could truly understand.

Rose sat in her armchair, tied her hair up, and put on her reading glasses. When she opened my first page, she found it blank. Where had the words gone? She frowned, wondering if perhaps I was just an empty journal she had mistaken for a book. But as her fingers brushed over the page, words began to appear, as if woken by her touch. Not the jumbled, indecipherable text she had seen in the store, but clear, flowing script that seemed to have been written in her own handwriting.

I am the Book of the Unknown.
I am Anant,
and my authors, Aara and Vaani,
were magical, mystical beings.

As Rose read the first line, her breath caught. It wasn't just curiosity; it felt like a forgotten part of her was calling, stirring from some deep sleep. She lingered on the words, barely aware as the pages, once yellowed with age, turned pastel white under her gaze. Was this real? Or just her imagination? She quickly closed the book, staring at the cover, now transformed. What had once been a brown, worn hardcover was now a rich olive green, and the gilded edges glinted with a single word in gold: *Anant.*

Rose's heartbeat quickened. She had never experienced anything like this, yet she sensed that her touch had somehow awakened the book, shifting it into something entirely new. The very title seemed like a summons, a call to rediscover parts of herself she had abandoned over the years.

Gazing at the cover, Rose noticed intricate inscriptions of nature: trees, shrubs, and flowers she had never seen before. She traced her fingers along the designs. They felt as alive as anything in nature. It was like holding hands with someone she loved for the first time, a feeling of time suspended, of complete belonging.

Since she was young, nature had always been her refuge: the forests, hills, rivers, and mountains her sanctuary. Born and raised in a quiet hill town, she often roamed alone, her father away on work, her only company the mysteries of the wild. But she had learned to tune out the whispers in the forest, to blend into the ordinary world around her.

Now, as I watched her, I sensed she knew that this moment signalled change. Her time of hiding, of blending in, was coming to an end. The alarm clock of her soul was ringing, calling her to shed the ordinary and embrace the extraordinary that had always lived within her. She smiled, recognizing this as the sign she had been waiting for; permission to begin her true journey.

Chapter 2

As Rose opened the next page, the words shimmered faintly, as if waiting to be spoken aloud. She sensed an energy pulsing from the page; the words seemed to be seeping into her skin, dissolving the chaos that clouded her mind. Something shifted within her and the words started pouring out in composure, Rose never knew she had.

Here I stand not to question but to accept. Accept my past, present, and the future. My fate. My destiny. The path on which I have always found myself walking unexpectedly through lifetimes, I shall hold the belief that it is mine to tread. Not only have I chosen it myself, but I am also destined for it.
I am the magic I hold, and magic is what I create.

Shrugging off the feeling that someone was watching her, Rose straightened her shoulders but couldn't help but look around. The set of eyes looking back at her caught her gaze. Her own reflection seemed anew. The book in the hand of the girl in the mirror, standing at the end of her room, seemed to be exuding a warm light, a light that flowed into her hand and appeared to be transcending into her.

Rose looked at the passage before her:

Let Anant, the book you hold, guide you in remembering who you were... are and meant to be.
May the wind passing by make you privy to its

secrets. May it give you its strength to withstand the strongest currents, for you are the epitome of hope.
May the fire within you ignite the deepest desires and suppressed emotions, for those strong enough to face their demons become immune to the hurt they can cause.
May the land, the soil, the path you tread, always lead you towards your inner self and zeal to entangle the mysteries you hold within; for, not only do you hold the answers to every question which has kept you awake at night, you also hold the power to ease the struggles and worries of everyone around you.
May the blood in your veins always hold the strength to withstand the challenges you face, for the life of a Giver is never easy. May the serenity and peace water brings always stand firm within you and help you calm the chaos around.
My darling,
May this prayer lead you into the world you belong, where all the elements of nature and the energy surrounding you don't stop reminding you of how magical you are and what you are capable of."

As the final word left her lips, Rose felt a stirring, as if the book was breathing with her. The air thickened, the atmosphere almost expectant, as though something ancient, and powerful was about to begin. She turned the page, ready to uncover the story of *Aara* and *Vaani*, the two names that felt both foreign and inexplicably familiar, like distant memories waiting to return.

I am certain you understand how I feel at this moment. Rose is stepping into the world she was always meant to find, and I, merely a spectator, can do nothing but watch in awe at what's to come. She's captivated, drawn in so deeply that she can't put me down, no, not anymore. Like a lover bound by an unspoken connection, all I can do is open my heart, surrendering myself to reveal everything within. For her, I am an open book in the truest sense, and the story is only beginning.

As soon as she recited the words, the book began to glow, a warm light pulsing from its pages. Then, to her utter disbelief, it spoke. Rose was stunned. Her world felt like a waking dream, everything impossible somehow real.

"To you, I may seem just a book of magic. A magic you've always sensed within yourself, yet ignored, forgotten over the years. But to me, Rose, you are my purpose, the very reason of my existence. I've waited for you across countless pages and moments. My name is Anant, and within me are answers to questions you've longed to resolve. It may feel overwhelming, I know. But in the story of Aara and Vaani, you will find the wisdom you seek, the guidance to remember who you are and all that you are capable of."

Rose sat back as she felt the weight of this revelation. Part of her wanted to close the book and run, but another part, a part deep inside her, felt this was where she was meant to be.

"No, my dear," Anant continued, sensing her hesitation. *"Don't look so shocked. I know it's a lot to take in, having a talking book right under your fingertips... it must seem as unreal as it feels."*

Rose gently set the book down, her gaze drifting to the mirror across the room, as if she almost needed to reassure herself that she was awake and not sleepwalking, lost in some hallucination brought on by exhaustion.

"Now, now, don't look so distressed," Anant comforted her. *"I am here, as real as you believe me to be. If proof is what you need from me... I shall abide."*

In that instant, her phone buzzed. Glancing down, she saw her father's name, an unexpected call from a man who hadn't reached out in years, not since her mother's passing and the fracture in their family. Her only connection with him had been a monthly envelope she sent, ensuring that fresh flowers adorned her mother's grave.

Heart pounding, Rose picked up the phone. She spoke to him softly, her tone tentative yet curious. Her father, too, sounded different. He confessed to the urge in his heart to talk to her. Inquiring about her well-being, his voice carried the warmth and tenderness that Rose had heard after years.

Unable to hold small talk and failing to suppress the emotions of guilt and regret boiling inside him, her father apologized. He admitted his shortcomings, years of stifled emotions, his cowardice, and the fear, and pain of seeing his daughter face-to-face. Rose wrapped her arms around herself and forgave him in her heart.

With tears still wet on her face, Rose assured her father that the past was behind them. She was fine, happy even. As she set down the phone, a sense of unexpected peace washed over her.

Turning back to *Anant,* her heart felt light, and warm in a way she hadn't felt in years. She took a deep breath, ready to embrace whatever this journey would bring.

"Yes," she whispered aloud. *"Magic comes to those who believe. If your name is truly Anant, then help me find myself, for I am weary of being lost."*

And in that moment, the book seemed to glow even brighter, as if to say: *This is only the beginning.*

Sometimes belief is all you need, not only to fully recognize but also to accept yourself.

Chapter 3

In the world from which I come, names carry more than mere syllables. They hold a purpose, and each name is a mirror, reflecting one's essence. Rose, what you are about to read is not simply names but symbols of power and guidance, each with a role in awakening a part of you. I hope that as you read and absorb what has been written for you, you may begin to see them not as characters but as pieces of a larger truth, keys that may one day unlock your own path. Let me share with you the story of Aara, a magical soul, and Vaani, the voice who nurtured her belief and kept her spirit alive.

Trusting Anant, Rose carefully opened to the first chapter, 'Aara and Vaani: Two Souls, One Journey.' The words on the page began to shift, swirling into shapes, and colours until they transformed into vibrant, moving images. The pages seemed to come alive, scenes unfolding before her as if she were gazing through a window into another world. Anant's voice deepened with a timeless warmth, guiding her into the story. The forest appeared, lush and teeming with life, and within its embrace, she saw a young girl, Aara, running freely, her laughter echoing through the trees. Rose felt herself being pulled into the scene, sensing the faint scent of earth and wildflowers, as though she, too, were stepping into this vivid, enchanting world.

"Aara was unlike the others," Anant began, his voice resonant yet soft, as if it held secrets that had waited lifetimes to be told. *"An outcast, set apart from her tribe, not by choice, but by nature. The sixth daughter in a family that longed for a son. Her quiet defiance*

went mostly unnoticed, giving her countless chances to slip away into the woods. There, she was free from the eyes that could never see her true spirit."

In the pages, Aara's figure wove gracefully through the trees, each step light as though the earth knew her well. Her eyes sparkled with a quiet wonder, a reflection of the strength she carried within.

"She was only eight when the echo in her mind revealed itself," Anant continued, *"the gentle voice of Vaani, a guiding light sent from above to keep her grounded in a world that did not understand her."*

Rose's eyes widened as she watched young Aara turn her face to the sky, lying peacefully on the grass, her fingers twirling the dried leaves with a flick. She felt a thrill as Anant's words grew more intimate, as if drawing her closer to the heart of the story.

"Aara always knew she was different," Anant whispered, a touch of pride in his tone. *"While others might have called her 'odd,' she felt, in her very core, that she was a pure creation of the earth, her spirit woven into the fabric of nature itself. With every breath she took, she believed that magic was her birthright. And on her eighth birthday, when Vaani's voice stirred in her mind, it empowered her to see herself as she truly was."*

With each line, Rose could feel Aara's awakening as though it were her own. Aara opened her eyes, gazing at her shimmering fingertips, trailing light in the air, an energy that pulsed with life.

"Magic is not something given," Anant intoned softly, his voice a guide, *"it is something realized, waiting within those who believe in it."*

Rose's heart raced. She could feel Aara's courage, her untamed connection with nature, as if she herself were stepping into that boundless belief. With each word Anant shared, the magic within Rose felt just a little more real.

Aara's love for stories was a quiet rebellion against the limits set by her world. In her family of poor farmers, books were scarce, and very few girls were taught to read or understand the wisdom within them. But Aara was different; her curiosity was boundless. Her mother, who had once been the daughter of a palace librarian, understood this hunger well. When she became the mother of six daughters, her father's love for knowledge proved invaluable. She now had stories and teachings she shared with her children. She saw the same spark in Aara's eyes that she once had herself, a spark she was determined not to let die.

Beside her mother or wandering alone in the forest with Vaani's quiet presence, Aara found her truest teachers. Though her life was simple, the voice of the forest filled her with understanding and whispered secrets that no one else seemed to hear. As her eldest sister's marriage approached, an unsettling truth began to unfold within her. The forest seemed to murmur warnings. Shadows of past brides lingered in the air, and Aara sensed a dark intention veiled behind the groom's family's smiles. Vaani's presence confirmed her intuition: this family sought brides only for dowry, with no trace left of those who had come before.

The voice of the trees, the very earth beneath her feet, seemed to echo an ancient warning only she could hear, urging her to protect her sister.

Aara confided in her mother, sharing the dark truth as best as she could. Though her mother believed her, the rest of the family dismissed her fears, deeming them the hysteria of a woman who had failed to bear a son. Helpless, they watched the marriage proceed as planned. Heartbroken, Aara realized that in her world, the voice of a woman had little worth. She vowed to grow strong enough that her voice would one day be heard.

After the wedding rites concluded and her sister prepared to depart with her husband, Aara pulled her aside. She spoke of an ancestral blessing that required her sister's return in six lunar cycles, a tradition vital for their family's harmony. The superstitious groom's family, unnerved by the ritual's importance, reluctantly agreed. To protect her sister further, Aara touched her forehead, exhaling a silent breath to awaken her sister's inner wisdom. *"Listen to your voice,"* she whispered, *"and trust any doubt that may stir within you."* In that quiet blessing, Aara passed on a part of herself, a connection to the pulse of the earth, the strength of the water, and the quiet vigilance of the night. Each step her sister took away from the village would carry Aara's protection, bound by faith in the voice within.

With her mother, Aara gathered water each night beneath the moonlight, offering it to the earth and praying for her sister's safe return. She knew now that this communion with nature, this silent dialogue with the elements, was where her actual strength lay... a power she would learn to wield, not just for herself, but for all those she loved.

When the lunar cycles came full circle, Aara's sister returned home, her spirit alight with gratitude as she sought out Aara. "Thank you," she said, her eyes shimmering with sincerity, "for blessing me with the voice that guided me through my days." She recounted how she had evaded the milk her mother-in-law brought each night and the treacherous paths into the dark forests they had urged her to tread. In those woods, she found refuge, often returning home to face the disappointment etched on her in-laws' faces. Yet, amidst the uncertainty, a flicker of hope ignited in her heart. Her husband had embraced her each night, his warmth wrapping around her like a protective cloak.

A week into their return, joy, and disbelief collided when Aara's sister learned she was pregnant. Her husband, upon hearing the news, wept openly, his heart swelling with a newfound love and responsibility. In the stillness of the night, he began to whisper promises of protection, feeling deep within himself that it was time for his penance. The realization of his past wrongdoings weighed heavily on him, igniting a fierce determination to protect his wife and their unborn child from any harm that might come their way.

This was the moment when Aara, her mother, and her sister recognized the truth held within the whispers of intuition. The voice that had guided them was a beacon of wisdom, illuminating their path even in darkness. Trust became their anchor, allowing them to navigate the tumultuous waters of life with newfound resilience.

As time flowed, Aara openly expressed her love for the rituals of water and fire, sharing her visions with her mother. *"Trust me,"* she implored, *"do not question the ways of the elements. I will protect our family, for we are bound by the strength of nature itself."* Through her connection with the earth, Aara knew that knowledge, and love would guide them all towards a brighter, safer future.

As the chapter drew to a close, Rose caught a glimpse of Aara sitting serenely in the woods, a gentle smile gracing her lips as if to reassure her. With a soft sigh, Rose closed the book, cradling it in her right hand while resting her left over her heart, feeling the warmth of newfound possibilities within her. *"Anant,"* she murmured, *"I remember how playing with water always calmed my worries. I wish to try the water ritual for my father's well-being. Even though we haven't spoken in years, my heart holds only the wish for him to be alright."*

The book resonated with her words, and Anant's voice filled the silence, warm, and reassuring. *"Goodnight, Rose,"* he said. *"You have opened the door to a mystical world, one that may bring with it new challenges and fears. Remember, with great power comes great responsibility. Trust in your inner strength, for it will guide you through the uncertainties ahead and help you confront the demons that await."*

As she settled into a peaceful slumber, Rose understood that this was merely the beginning of her journey. With each turning page, she would learn to embrace the magic within herself, knowing that faith, and courage would light her way through whatever lay ahead.

The next morning, Rose woke with a feeling of renewed energy, a quiet hum coursing through her. It's the nature of true understanding, she thought. Once you see yourself clearly, what you are, and all you're capable of, it stirs a spark within you that's impossible to ignore. She caught a glimpse of herself in the mirror and saw a brightness there, an unfamiliar glow that softened the tired lines around her eyes and replaced them with a quiet, hopeful light.

She dressed slowly, savouring this sense of ease, and then walked over to her reading corner where the magical book lay. Leaning down, she touched its cover with reverence, almost as if to confirm that yesterday's experience had been real. Just then, Anant's calm voice spoke, "Yes, my dear, I am real." A smile broke across her face, and she murmured, "I was almost afraid it was all a dream."

Reassured, she felt a warmth rising from her heart, a gentle certainty that today would be different. She lifted her bag with a new sense of purpose, her eyes bright as she spoke aloud, "Today, I will find my reason for being where I am. I'll discover how to use the knowledge I've gained over the years, and I'll bring my whole self to it."

As she stepped outside, the first morning rays touched her skin, and Rose paused, feeling them seep into her very core. The warmth filled her like a gentle wave, spreading through her like a quiet happiness emanating from within. Was this the beauty of truly understanding oneself? She had never felt so open, so attuned to everything around her, the sunlight, the soft murmur of the trees, the gentle rustling of leaves. It was as if she and nature were breathing in time, each heartbeat a promise of magic, of possibilities.

Anant, watching quietly, wished for her nothing but days filled with this same joy, a happiness born from knowing one's own worth and letting it shine.

Rose's footsteps led her to a small, dimly lit office. The basement workspace of a local magazine, tucked under the hum of the post office. When she'd first accepted the junior editor role, she'd felt a glimmer of hope, a step towards something bigger. But years had passed, and now the shabby office, with its stale air, and low hum of fluorescent lights, seemed more like a reminder of dreams deferred. The endless cycle of proofreading trivial articles and managing tedious tasks had worn her down. Her initial ambition, to channel her voice, and make a difference, felt distant, nearly out of reach. The job she once welcomed as an opportunity to rise above her past had instead become a place where her spirit felt trapped and her aspirations stalled in the shadows.

Growing up, life may have felt simpler to Rose in some ways, but it was far from easy. As a child, she found a measure of comfort in her mother's presence, yet the burdens on them were heavy. Each morning, she rose early to let the cows graze before school, only to return home, and dive into a list of chores. Her father was often away for work, leaving her mother to shoulder not only their own responsibilities but also the relentless demands of relatives next door. These family members assumed that Rose's mother, who worked long hours at a local chemist, had time, and energy to spare. They relied on her as unpaid help for cleaning, cooking, and caring for their children, in turn burdening Rose with endless expectations. Treated as little more than extra labour, Rose faced exhaustion without anyone to defend or comfort her.

Despite the hardships, Rose held on to two certainties: the desire to become someone who mattered and the hope of lifting her mother out of a life of unending servitude. But fate had other plans. When Rose was fifteen, her mother caught a flu that spiralled quickly into something far worse. The cruel irony of working in a chemist's shop yet lacking the resources for proper care was not lost on Rose. In only three months, the illness took away her mother, stripping Rose of her one steadfast anchor and any semblance of stability.

In her final days, Rose's mother tried to impart all the wisdom she could. She shared hard-won insights from years of sacrifice and endurance, from being a wife who took on household duties alone to accepting the isolation of her husband's absence. Watching her mother's quiet strength, Rose was profoundly shaped by her example. She understood that, from this point on, she had to protect herself. Her mother's resilience had taught her one invaluable lesson: that strength came not from avoiding hardship but from facing it head-on.

Determined to honour her mother's legacy, Rose spent the next two years focused on her education, eventually renting a small cottage on the outskirts of the village to be closer to college and far from the constant demands of her extended family. In that space, Rose discovered a profound truth: financial independence gave her the power to make her own choices. Unlike her mother, who had quietly accepted her fate, Rose saw a path to freedom, one paved by self-reliance. After finishing her schooling, Rose left her village and stepped into the city, determined to create a life on her own terms, one that no longer bore the weight of others' expectations.

As Rose stepped into the office that morning, she felt a shift within; a lighter, renewed sense of purpose. Her first instinct was to smile, a genuine warmth that hadn't surfaced in a long time. She greeted her coworkers on her way to her desk and asked if anyone wanted coffee, breaking her usual quiet routine. Mr. Bari, the elderly guard in his late seventies, noticed the change in her usual self. His weathered face softened as he approached her desk.

"You look like yourself today, Miss Rose," he said with a gentle, comforting voice. "I don't know what's changed, but it's good to see you this way. You're different, better than most around here. I hope you keep finding yourself." He placed a rough but reassuring hand on her head, a blessing of sorts, before he returned to his chair.

Rose felt tears prick her eyes. Mr.. Bari's words lingered with her, echoing a promise she'd made to herself: to see life from a fresh perspective. She looked back on all the times he'd watched over her quietly since she first came to this place. Though they hadn't spoken much, she'd often sensed his kind presence, like a guardian. Thinking of her own journey, she suddenly felt compelled to reach out, crossing a barrier of her usual shyness. She walked over to him and asked about his family, about why he rarely took time off to visit them.

Mr.. Bari shared a bit of his life, explaining that his modest salary helped keep his family afloat. For years, he'd sent regular cheques back to his village, believing it was enough to care for them. He had long accepted that he would live alone here, away from the warmth of his family. As he spoke, Rose felt a tug on her heart. She knew what it was like to grow up without a parent at home. Money alone couldn't replace the presence of a loved one.

"Mr. Bari, I hope you get a chance to be with them soon," she said softly. Remembering something she'd read the night before, she gently blew on his hand, like Aara, hoping to bring him a small blessing. "I hope you find your way back to them. Sometimes, presence is what matters most."

Just then, the phone on her desk rang, pulling her back to reality. She excused herself and returned to her desk to answer. It was her editor, calling to report a fire near the mechanic's shop in the east wing and asked Rose to cover the story. Unexpectedly, he also requested that she bring Mr. Bari along, since his home was in the affected area. Rose felt her heart sink as she relayed the news to Mr. Bari.

His face drained of colour, and for a moment, he looked as though the strength had left his body. She helped him stand, reassuring him softly, "I'm sure it'll be okay. We'll get there soon. Everything will work out."

When they arrived, firefighters had nearly brought the blaze under control, but the damage was severe. The garage and two neighbouring homes had been reduced to charred remnants. Mr. Bari's modest belongings, his years of quiet, hardworking life, had all turned to dust. Only a few items remained: a family portrait he had taken with him years ago and a couple of spare clothes.

In the days that followed, Mr. Bari's employer, and the police assured him that the fire was an accident and that insurance would cover the damages. But until repairs were made, he would need to find temporary accommodation. Though his employer granted him leave to manage the transition, Rose couldn't shake the sadness she felt for him. She worried that now, more than ever, Mr. Bari might feel resigned to postpone his long-awaited visit home.

But to her surprise, Mr. Bari's resolve remained intact. Calm and steady, he shared the news with her one afternoon, a soft light in his eyes. "I've booked my train ticket home," he said, smiling gently. "Thank you, Rose. You helped me remember what really matters."

As Rose watched him leave that day, she realized that perhaps, in a small way, she had helped him find his own path back to his family, just as she was finding her way back to herself.

Rose began to spend more time with her colleagues, weaving herself into the fabric of their lives by learning their stories and, in turn, sharing pieces of her own. The office felt less like a place of work and more like a community. Laughter punctuated her conversations, and she seemed brighter, livelier, almost as if the weight on her shoulders had started to lift.

In the evenings, her time was devoted to Aara, Vaani, and Anant. They became her guides, teaching her about ancient fire and water rituals, practices meant to awaken inner strength and fortify the spirit. Each night, Rose would open the book, feeling the slight resistance of the worn pages, and continue where she had left off. The moment she turned to the right page, she would find Aara waiting for her in the heart of the forest, eyes alight with that familiar welcoming smile, as Anant's voice wove stories through the crisp air.

Small moments and gestures within the story spoke volumes, carrying Rose deeper into Aara's world. She traced the journey of the girl whose bond with the elements mirrored her own search for balance. When Aara turned sixteen, the world around her seemed to shift ominously. Her older sisters were married off, and the air buzzed with talk of her own future. Yet, Aara belonged not to the conventions of domestic life but to the wilderness, to the trees, the soil, and the winding river. She was a part of the woods, a soul intertwined with the whispers of leaves and the heartbeat of the earth.

But Aara's connection with nature also marked her as different. To the villagers, she was the strange one, the girl with a witch's aura. Her father had struggled for years to find a suitor who would take her as she was, haunted by rumours, and tales woven from ignorance. Yet Aara found solace in her solitude, content in the forest's embrace.

However, life's moments of peace are often fleeting, shadowed by oncoming trials. Dark clouds began to gather at the edges of Aara's cherished woods, casting a chill through the air and stirring an instinctual sense of foreboding. It was as if the trees whispered warnings. Aara knew then, change was coming, and she needed to be prepared for whatever storms lay ahead.

The boy came from a faraway village, but tales of his commanding presence had already reached Aara's town. Her father's voice carried a note of hope when he spoke about him. A strong-willed, principled young man who stood unwaveringly by his beliefs, unafraid to challenge the world for what he deemed right. Unlike the others, her father believed, this boy would not succumb to the town's whispers about Aara. Once he met her and saw her beauty, he would surely choose to stand by her.

Aara, now blooming like a pure rose on the verge of blossoming, held an allure her family likened to something deserving of a warrior's devotion. Little did they know, her strength lay deep within, capable of weathering storms without needing rescue. Reluctantly, Aara resigned herself to meeting this stranger, even as the idea churned unease in her heart. The preparations were made, and the boy was summoned.

Vaani tried to reassure Aara, her words like a gentle breeze carrying resolve. *"Trust in yourself, no matter where life's path leads. You have me, and the wind, soil, water, and fire as your guides. Living among people is part of being human, but remember that your spirit remains unyielding. You will endure."*

The boy, Aameen, arrived with two friends, rugged in appearance. He came from a large family but had long distanced himself due to his resolute, unconventional way of life. He stood tall, six feet, with well-defined arms bearing fresh bruises from an encounter on his journey. Word had it, he was known for defending the defenceless, be it person, or beast. His black-olive eyes and unruly, dusty brown hair framed a face that was both fierce and unexpectedly captivating. Despite his rough exterior, Aara found herself drawn to his quiet intensity during their first meeting.

Aameen, on the other hand, felt an almost magnetic pull to Aara, whom the villagers had warned him about, calling her a "green witch". But standing there, he saw only a vision: eyes of deep teal that seemed to reach into his very soul, hair cascading like spun bronze to her waist, and limbs so delicate they appeared untouched by toil. She seemed otherworldly, almost as if the earth itself cradled her footsteps. He could only think, *what a rare, untouched beauty she is.*

The family played their parts with practised ease, their behaviour a carefully orchestrated display. They believed Aameen might be their last hope for Aara, the youngest daughter marked by rumour and misunderstood by most. Aameen, enchanted by her, and moved by the family's genuine affection, agreed to the marriage, stipulating that he wanted no dowry, only Aara, and her simple belongings.

As Aameen prepared to leave, he realized he hadn't spoken to Aara directly, not beyond a glimpse of her when he first arrived. The thought struck him as odd. He turned to her father and asked for a brief conversation, reasoning that they would share a life, and he wanted to understand her beyond the fleeting look.

Aara's father hesitated, tension creasing his brow. He feared an inauspicious event that might shatter the fragile hope they had built. Yet, he consented, and sent Aara's mother to accompany Aameen to the oak tree where Aara often sought solace.

Towering trees shadowed the short walk, and Aameen's admiration only deepened. Aara's courage to dwell alone in such a place fascinated him. Before they reached the tree house, Aara's mother turned to him, her eyes glistening.

"Aameen, my daughter is more than what you see. She holds the spirit of the earth and sky, a guardian in her own right. Marrying her is not just about gaining a wife, but about finding a guiding star. She will protect you in ways you cannot imagine. Love her for who she is, and never, I beg you, try to mould her into anything less than what she was born to be."

Moved by her words, Aameen's voice softened. He promised, "I will be her companion, her shield, if need be, but I will never change who she is." He realized then that he did not need to speak to Aara that day. The conviction in her mother's plea was enough. Respecting Aara's space, he requested to return, vowing he would wait until Aara was ready.

From the tree house, Aara had overheard the exchange. A pang of guilt pricked her heart. *Had she misjudged him? Had she been too quick to assume?* She wondered, as the forest around her seemed to breathe with new possibilities.

The days leading up to the wedding were both frenetic and surreal for Aara. She immersed herself in the unfamiliar routines of household chores, each task an act of quiet surrender. Aara, once a free spirit of the forest, was now the dutiful daughter, a tribute to the mother who had nurtured her. Bound by love, duty, and a sense of foreboding, she adhered to the rules instilled by her father, each instruction woven with threads of sacrifice and obedience. In her eyes lingered a fragile hope that Aameen would be the person she believed he could be, a hope bolstered by the words he had spoken to her mother. *How fragile we are as humans*, she thought. *A single moment can spark trust, while another can ignite doubt.*

The days of preparation were marked by a bittersweetness. Aara practised the rhythms of what life as a wife in another's home would demand, forcing herself to adapt to the unfamiliar roles and gestures. The simplicity of the wedding was a nod to Aameen's wishes, but Aara's family, despite their limited means, spared no effort to meet the subtle expectations of the boy's kin. The ceremonies were swift, lasting only two days. Yet, those days marked the end of a chapter and the beginning of another that filled Aara with both anticipation and silent dread.

On the eve of her departure, a storm of emotions swirled within her. She felt a sudden, irrepressible urge to seek solace in the only place that had ever understood her; the heart of the forest, with its sentinel, the great oak tree. Disregarding propriety and the newly imposed bounds of marriage, Aara slipped out into the night, her steps hurried as if guided by an unseen hand. The air was thick with the whispering of leaves, and the wind seemed to mourn her impending departure.

Reaching the oak, she flung her arms around the ancient trunk, the rough bark pressing into her cheek like the embrace of an old friend. A familiar voice, rooted in the essence of the tree, spoke to her, "My child, my dear, dear child. You step now into the next chapter of your journey. Remember the teachings that ground you. You are not just of the earth; you are its very heart, its mother. You are the source of life's energy and the quiet that comes at the end of it. Wherever you go, let joy follow. But remember, the bright morning skies will always have their shadows, for light, and darkness are bound together. In times of darkness, remember who you are; in the light, live what you know to be true. Claim your power, as the land, the wind, the fire, and the water are part of you, as you are part of them."

Aara's heart, marked with this final blessing, thudded with sorrow, and resolve. Tears welled in her eyes as she pressed her palm to the bark one last time. With a final glance at her sanctuary, she turned away, the weight of the unknown pressing against her chest like an iron hand.

Back in the present, Rose listened to Anant's voice as he narrated Aara's parting from her beloved forest. The vision of Aara, tear-streaked, and full of unspoken fears, made Rose's own heart clench. She couldn't bear the possibility of Aara suffering the same fate she had. A sudden rush of memories overwhelmed her, past moments of shattered trust and the bitter sting of love's betrayal. She shut the book with trembling hands, unable to let the story continue.

"Anant," she whispered, her voice breaking, "I can't bear to listen if something goes wrong for Aara. She looked so broken, so lost. I know the agony of leaving a home, of being torn from the only life you know, to step into an uncertain world that promises nothing. I've been there, with a heart full of love, only to have it shattered. What if Aameen isn't the man he seemed to be? What if Aara's hopes are just as fragile as mine were?"

A single tear slid down her cheek, and soon others followed, each one a testament to the wounds still raw in her heart.

It was soon after her mother's death that Rose realized the only way to free herself was through higher education and financial independence. It took time, but she eventually convinced her extended family to support her decision. She wrote a letter to her father, informing him of her choice, despite knowing he would disapprove. By the time she had made that decision, however, Rose had grown isolated, her heart heavy with loneliness. She knew she was on her own in this world, and she would have to look after herself.

Then came a guy with his charming, frisky behaviour. Someone who found her distant demeanour fascinating, her detachment from the world tempting. He was drawn to her betrayal of everything that seemed important to others. Rose didn't speak to anyone, but he slowly inched his way into her life. People with fragile egos often prey on those who lack self-belief, and over time, he gained her trust. Small gestures, asking about her day, her health, or if she was eating right, became routine. It was the first time someone had shown that kind of care since her mother, and Rose, starved for affection, began to warm to him.

In her innocence, she began trusting him. When he first touched her, a chill ran through her, but she ignored it, too desperate for connection to heed the warning. Over time, as he became more persistent in his advances, Rose tried to maintain her distance, but he grew distant. He told her she didn't trust him fully, that he was smitten with her, and that he would do anything to earn her trust. Fearful of losing the only person who had shown any mercy towards her, Rose lowered her guard.

Though deep down, her instincts screamed at her to be careful, Rose, deprived of love, and affection, made the mistake of letting him in. What followed was a painful affair. At first, he seemed caring, but his true nature soon emerged. As he realized she was emotionally dependent on him, he grew more aggressive, and demanding. Arguments became frequent, and within months, the relationship turned violent. He would hit her, and Rose's quiet submission only fuelled his anger.

In the darkness of this toxic relationship, she tried to hold onto her sense of self. Towards the end of her college days, he told her they would move to his village, and he wanted to marry her as soon as he found a job. Fearful for her life and her future, Rose finally snapped. The night after her last exam, she took the train, and vanished without a trace. She didn't tell anyone, no teachers, no family, where she was going, too terrified to let anyone know where she could be found.

The days and nights spent in fear, always wondering if he would track her down, pushed Rose into a shell so deep that even she couldn't have predicted it. Whatever small hope she had for happiness seemed to disappear as quickly as her sense of safety. It wasn't until she started working in the years that followed that the fear began to fade, though the scars on her heart would never fully heal.

Seeing Aara's fear and hearing about her struggles reignited the terror Rose thought she had buried. The familiar unease crept back into her bones, and she could feel herself unravelling once again.

Anant had always known that Rose's life couldn't have been simple. The lives of those who are deeply attuned to emotions rarely are. Their heightened ability to understand both their own feelings and those of others makes them vulnerable to hurt and disappointment. This heightened sensitivity not only intensifies their emotions but also tends to draw negative energy and people into their orbit.

As Rose opened up about her past, she spoke of people who always looked out for themselves. She hesitated to label them as selfish, but to someone like her, who struggled to say no or set boundaries, that's exactly how it felt. For those with low self-esteem, like Rose once was, such encounters were devastating. It wasn't that they didn't feel pain. It was that they didn't know how to express or manage their emotions effectively. And then some exploited this vulnerability, channelling their own hidden insecurities through aggression and manipulation.

Rose shared her belief that Aara, despite her strong personality, had never faced real conflict. At least not in the way Rose had. Anant listened intently, piecing together Rose's emotions, and understanding her perspective.

"Rose," Anant began gently, "you need to give Aara the benefit of the doubt. Strength isn't something she was born with; it's something she built over time. She stood her ground to prove her worth and knew the difference between right and wrong. Yes, she's at a turning point, joining a new family where no one truly knows her or sees her potential. But listening to her story is important because it teaches us how challenges come and go, and what remains are the lessons we learn from them. Even if situations break someone, it's up to that person to choose which pieces to leave behind and which to gather to rebuild themselves."

"You might not have noticed, but when Aara reached her new home, she did everything she could to adapt. She faced backlash for her beliefs and her way of life, but slowly, and steadily, she found her footing. The village may have been unfamiliar, but it was surrounded by forests, fresh soil, and rivers, the constancy of nature. Aara understood that, no matter how foreign her surroundings felt, nature's support was unwavering. The inner power she possessed wouldn't disappear overnight. It's essential to acknowledge what she endured because those hardships are as much a part of her character as her triumphs. They deserve recognition."

Anant's words resonated with Rose. He was right. She, too, had been shaped by everything she had faced, even the lonely nights spent crying into the darkness. Every experience counted, contributing to the person she had become.

Rose reopened the book and turned to the next page, where a dark sky loomed over Aara. A gentle breeze brushed against her as she gazed up, seeking guidance from Vaani.

"What happened to her?" Rose asked, her curiosity piqued.

"Aameen requested her company for a journey that could last months with no certain return date," Anant explained. "He didn't want to leave Aara behind, knowing she struggled to fit in despite her best efforts. Societal norms are constructed to break the spirit of those who don't conform."

Anant went on to describe how, just the day before, Aara had discovered she was pregnant. Now she stood at a crossroads, deciding whether to reveal this news to Aameen or embark on the journey and confess later. Telling Aameen might change everything; he could insist she stay behind, or his family might ensure it, keeping her from the only support and love she had in him. But if she chose to go and something happened to the unborn child, how could she face Aameen? How would she forgive herself?

Vaani understood Aara's deepest fears: losing the life she shared with Aameen, especially now that she was carrying his child. Raising the baby alone in a world that knew nothing of her and would neither accept nor support her independence felt insurmountable. Meanwhile, as Aameen spoke of the journey and the places they would visit, the wind that touched him, the soil beneath his feet, and the trees embracing the village sensed his impending absence. This foreknowledge kept Aara awake for nights, her mind racing.

In the end, the answer seemed straightforward. Had she discovered the pregnancy mid-journey, she would have continued without hesitation. With her heart and mind weighed down by deliberation, Aara finally told Aameen of her decision: she would stay by his side and embark on the journey as the companion he had asked for.

Aameen was overjoyed when Aara agreed to accompany him. The thought of sharing his journey with his life companion filled him with happiness. It was a wonderful feeling to know that Aara, the one he cherished deeply but hadn't yet confessed his love to, would be by his side to experience each moment. He could now be himself, sharing both the highs, and the lows with the one he truly loved. This anticipation of their shared adventure lit a spark within him, making every step feel more significant and meaningful. Aameen was a remarkable man, kind, and principled, standing out among the men in his village for his decency. He admired Aara for her innocence and the unique perspective she brought to everything. Though Aameen had a tough exterior, he was deeply sensitive at heart. However, his fierce opposition to those who oppressed the less fortunate had earned him many enemies. While only a few influential individuals held enough influence to cause real harm, there were always those ready to act on their behalf, waiting for an excuse to crush anyone who dared to challenge their authority.

They believed this was the natural order, a law of dominance. Aameen rejected this notion. He thought everyone deserved freedom and a life of dignity. Aara deeply respected Aameen for his principles and unwavering commitment to protecting the vulnerable. He had a profound impact on the lives of people he barely knew, often lending a helping hand without hesitation. Whatever Aameen earned or collected from the wild, he divided carefully: 50 per cent for his family, 25 per cent set aside for those in need, and the remainder shared between himself and his companions who travelled with him to trade his beautifully crafted goods. It was striking to know that beneath his rugged exterior, Aameen was an artist at heart, renowned for the intricate, handmade carpets he created with the team that accompanied him on his journey.

It was three days into their journey, during which everyone was riding on horseback, that Aara began to feel unwell. Unaware of the risks associated with early pregnancy, she didn't realize that riding could be harmful. Aameen, attributing her discomfort to the change in environment and the strain of limited food and water, assumed she was simply unaccustomed to such travel. Nevertheless, driven by his instinct to care for her, he ordered the group to halt for a day so Aara could recover. By nightfall, her pallor showed no improvement, and Aameen's concern grew. He gently asked Aara if she could sense what might be wrong with her, as she often did with others. Seeing the worry in his eyes, Aara confessed that she believed she might be pregnant.

Aameen was stunned, his eyes wide with a mix of joy and anxiety. The news filled him with a rush of emotions, ecstatic delight tempered by worry, knowing Aara had been riding a horse for three days. Composing himself, he embraced her tightly, and Aara could feel his heart racing. She reassured him that she believed the baby was fine, but she felt weak, and would need to rest for at least two more days. Aameen agreed and informed their companions of the situation, suggesting that they continue ahead while he and Aara followed at a slower pace. His friends, who had known him since childhood, were thrilled for him, and offered to stay behind. However, Aameen insisted it wasn't necessary; he and Aara would manage on their own. After heartfelt congratulations from the group, his companions set off at sunrise, leaving Aameen, and Aara to move at a pace that would allow her to regain her strength.

It had been a glorious two months filled with Aameen and Aara spending their days and nights together, deepening their bond, and learning more about each other. Aameen had successfully sold all the carpets his cart carried, yet restlessness gnawed at him due to the lack of news from his friends. They were supposed to meet the rest of the troop a month ago, but there was no sign of them. Aameen had visited three villages that his friends were expected to pass through, but to his disappointment, none of the villagers had heard from them. Hoping for their safety, Aameen reached out to his contacts in and around the villages, asking them to keep him informed of any updates.

With the help of his cousin, Aameen managed to acquire a few new carpets to sell in the upcoming villages that he and his troop planned to visit. Although there had never been an instance where any member of the group had gotten lost in the forest, Aameen couldn't shake off a growing sense of dread. He hoped it was merely a matter of lost direction and not a sign of something more dire. Despite not being an official leader, Aameen was deeply respected, and naturally looked up to by his mates. He felt an overwhelming sense of responsibility for their safety.

After much thought, he decided to share his concerns with Aara, recalling what her mother had once told him—that Aara possessed the power to protect and keep her loved ones safe. While he didn't put much stock in the idea of magic, Aara had always carried an aura of mysticism around her, and now Aameen hoped she could offer some insight about his friends.

Aara listened intently, her eyes reflecting the worry she sensed in Aameen. Though he had tried to mask it over the past month, she could now discern the source of the tension that had been radiating from him.

"Keep patience and try not to worry, Aameen. I will do my best to find out what happened and where your friends might be," Aara said softly.

Hearing her words, Aameen felt a flicker of scepticism. How could Aara possibly gather such information? Yet, he chose to place his trust in the woman he loved. He nodded, feeling a wave of unexpected calm wash over him. "You should rest, Aameen," she added, noticing the fatigue etched on his face. Realizing how exhausted he truly was, Aameen agreed. For the first time in days, he felt a glimmer of hope that answers might soon come.

Aara waited until Aameen had fallen asleep before stepping quietly into the forest. She settled on the grass with a pot of water in her lap. With a gentle swirl of her fingers, she traced circles on the water's surface. A shimmering, glittering pulse radiated from her touch, and the water seemed to glow, coming alive under her spell. A soft breeze rustled the leaves, brushing her shoulders as she whispered her worries to the wind—their friends missing, the troop unaccounted for in the dense forest.

The wind, now mingling with the magic-infused water, carried her message away. Tiny droplets lifted from the pot, glowing faintly as they scattered in all directions, riding the currents of air to seek out any sign of their lost companions. Aara closed her eyes, reciting prayers to the elements, invoking the spirit of life and nature. She waited, heart pounding, until the droplets returned, merging back into the pot and swirling rapidly.

When Aara opened her eyes, she gasped at the vision within

the water. Crimson red, like blood, streaked through the liquid, and a muddy, soiled texture clung to her fingertips. She knew instantly where the group was, but dread seized her at the thought of telling Aameen.

At dawn, Aameen awoke to find Aara preparing a cup of herbal tea. She handed it to him and urged him to sit and listen. Without explaining her methods, she knew Aameen would struggle to comprehend them, she relayed the harsh truth. Something terrible had befallen their friends. They lay two feet beneath the ground to the west, their horses taken by the men who had killed them. Their deaths had been swift but cruel, and the forest warned of an unfaithful observer tracking their movements.

Rage coursed through Aameen at the news, but realization tempered his anger. He was no longer alone; he had Aara and their unborn child to consider. In the past, he would have sought immediate retribution, pursuing the murderers with reckless resolve. But now, the stakes were higher. Protecting his family became paramount, and any miscalculation could put them in danger.

The revelation that someone they knew might have betrayed them added a more profound unease. The thought gnawed at him as he carefully planned his next move. He turned to Aara, urging her to stay inside the cottage and lock the doors. Aara's eyes reflected the rising fear, knowing that being alone was fraught with its own dangers. She could defend herself, but the life growing inside her was another matter entirely.

Despite her misgivings, Aameen was resolute. He reassured her that he needed to seek out an old acquaintance in the last village for shelter and could not risk taking her into unknown territory. Aara felt a chill run down her spine, but accepted his plan. She would lock the door and practice protection spells, waiting anxiously for his return.

As the first rays of dawn painted the horizon, Aara once again urged to go with him. Aameen, however, believed it was safer for her to remain hidden. He knew that fear made them vulnerable, and he needed to keep that vulnerability far from those who sought to exploit it.

Aameen knew his routes well. As he left early in the morning, leaving Aara behind, his mind raced through the names of those he could reach out for help. Bhoomi Dev, the nearest village, seemed the best option, and within a couple of hours, he arrived there. With urgency, he sought out his childhood friend and explained the dire situation. When his friend heard the devastating news of the murders of Aameen's fellow travellers and the looming threat to his family, he didn't hesitate for a moment. Word spread quickly among the villagers, many of whom Aameen had helped over the years, some directly, others through quiet acts of kindness. Without a second thought, they rallied together to accompany him back to the forest, eager to support him in protecting his family and repay his courage and selflessness.

Not far from the cottage, they spotted the goons circling it, pounding on the door. Though Aameen's group was outnumbered, the drive to protect those they loved far surpassed the malice of their foes. The power to safeguard and preserve would always outweigh the will to destroy, that was nature's enduring rule.

Vaani was comforting Aara, urging her to hold on to faith in Aameen and his promise, when a sudden, jarring knock on the door startled her, causing her heart to leap into her throat. Fear surged through her, and without thinking, she darted under the cupboard, invoking a spell to cloak her presence. The knock turned to pounding, each heavy fist shaking the door, followed by cruel laughter echoing from outside. They knew she was there, and it was only a matter of time before they broke through.

The door splintered open, and chaos erupted, the room filled with shouts and the clash of bodies. Blood splattered across the floor, and Aara's pulse thundered in her ears. Then, amidst the uproar, she heard it, Aameen's voice, a cry filled with terror. The sound pierced her heart, shattering her concentration, and the spell she'd cast faltered and fell away.

Aara's eyes widened in horror as she stepped out, seeing a towering man pinning Aameen to the floor, his fist raised to strike. An ancient, untapped rage surged within her, boiling up through her chest. With a scream so powerful it shattered every window and glass in the cottage, she released a force that tore through the air. The assailants, friends and foes, alike, fell to the ground, clutching their heads in agony, as though their skulls were being shattered from within.

Tears streaked down Aara's face, her pain amplifying as she saw Aameen so vulnerable. The air around her sharpened, slicing through those who had dared to hurt him. She stopped screaming, her voice breaking into whispers as she walked towards Aameen. Protection spells slipped from her lips, barely audible through her sobs. A protective haze enveloped him, shielding him from the storm of her unleashed power.

Aameen looked around, shocked by the sight of his enemies writhing on the floor, hands covering their eyes, and ears. But a more profound terror gripped him when he noticed blood trickling from Aara's nose. She was pouring everything she had into shielding him, but at what cost? His gaze shifted to the dark stain spreading across her clothes—blood soaking her thighs.

Aara stumbled, collapsing into Aameen's arms, her body trembling with exhaustion. Her voice, weak but resolute, whispered an apology. "I had the choice to save only one," she said, her eyes brimming with sorrow. "And I will never be sorry for choosing you—not in this life, not in any other."

As Aara fainted into Aameen's arms, her power retreating into eerie silence, the men with him found new strength. They swiftly moved to get Aara and Aameen out of the crumbling chaos. The goons, who had already felt the sting of an unseen, powerful force, no longer stood a chance. One by one, they fell, either killed, or incapacitated, their malice torn from their bodies as though the very force of Aara's power had unravelled their existence. The few who survived fled, unable to withstand the fury of Aara's rage.

Aameen didn't pursue them. Their flight no longer mattered. Vengeance for the deaths of his friends could wait. What mattered now was Aara's safety, her life, and the precious life she carried. The only purpose that drove Aameen in that moment was to get her far away from the chaos, to a place of safety. The tale of that day spread across the village, of the higher power that had shielded the righteous and protected the innocent. It became an unspoken warning to anyone who dared challenge such love again.

It took Aara two weeks to regain consciousness, but she was still too weak to remain awake for long. Aameen stayed beside Aara's bed the entire time she was unconscious. The local *Dai*, the midwife, had been called immediately after their arrival at the safe house, but Aameen's worst fears were realized. Much to his sorrow, the Dai confirmed that the child couldn't have survived the strain Aara had put her body through. The Dai wasn't sure why, but she confided in Aameen that the reason had to be more significant than Aara's own life. "Even her life was at risk," she explained. "But something within her, some force, held her heart to keep breathing."

Aameen stood in silence, his heart heavy with the weight of the truth. He had hoped, he had prayed for a different outcome, but now all that mattered was Aara's survival. He would endure anything to see her alive again, to hold her once more, and to protect her from the pain of the past. His only hope now was that Aara would find the strength to live again, for both herself, and of the love they shared.

After three lunar cycles since the tragic incident, Aara finally opened her eyes and instinctively touched her abdomen. The grief was immediate, etched into the lines of her face. She was aware of her loss, and the weight of it pressed heavily on her. Turning her head slightly, she saw Aameen asleep beside her, exhaustion evident in his posture. It seemed to be the middle of the night, so she refrained from moving too much, afraid of waking him.

Aara's gaze drifted to the window, and she raised her hand, swirling her fingers to open it. A cool breeze swept into the room, brushing her face, and a solitary firefly floated inside, making its way to her outstretched hand. Just as the firefly settled on her forefinger, Vaani's gentle voice broke the silence.

"My dear, I know your pain runs too deep for words to mend. But hold on to your faith, in yourself, and in your husband, your partner through this storm. Aameen shares your sorrow; the loss is his as well. Remember, neither of you is to blame. Sometimes, life's cruelties defy reason. Humanity, in its complexity, often disrupts nature's balance, but destiny is unchangeable. Life requires sacrifice, and love demands protection.

"What you did was right. Even Mother Nature stood by you, sending vibrations through the earth to keep your heart beating. The loss of a child is an incomparable pain, boundless, and raw. But know this: if it is in your destiny, you will bear a child again. What is certain now is your duty to safeguard this land and the people within it. Use your energy for their good. The spells and magic you wielded at the hour of need took a significant part of you, but they also unlocked your last chakra, the supreme power that had long lain

dormant within you, forgotten amidst the daily demands of life.

"Now is the time, Aara, to rise to your true purpose. To remove your cloak and embrace your destiny. You have the power to heal, to protect those pure of heart, to uplift those who seek change. You are one with Mother Nature. But remember: a mother gives life; she does not take it. Guide those who have lost their way, and let the wandering souls find their own path back to you."

Aara's eyes filled with tears as Vaani's words settled deep within her, touching the raw edges of her grief and promising the possibility of healing. With a faint sense of hope for the days ahead, she closed her eyes, and drifted back into sleep.

Rose closed the book, feeling a mixture of grief for Aara's profound loss and comfort in knowing that she wasn't alone in her battle. Aameen stood steadfast by her side, a beacon of unwavering support. The room seemed to hold its breath as Rose absorbed the weight of the story, her fingers tracing the embossed edges of the book cover as if seeking solace in its solidity.

After a long, thoughtful silence, Anant spoke. His voice was gentle but firm, resonating with wisdom. "Every experience in life comes with a purpose, Rose. Whether it feels like a blessing or a burden, it's there to teach us something vital. Nights, with their shadows, are always followed by days, just as days full of lessons lead to nights of trials. It's through this cycle that life shapes us, sharpens us, and reveals our true purpose. Loss and devastation are part of what makes us human. Just like the brightest joys, they demand to be endured. And it is in enduring them that we learn resilience."

Rose felt the truth of his words settle into her heart like an anchor. She reflected on her own past, the losses she had endured, and how they had shaped her into who she was today. The trials she had faced weren't just isolated moments of suffering; they were stepping stones that prepared her for the hardships yet to come. Life, she realized, was a delicate balance, like yin and yang. Joy and sorrow, triumph, and failure, each played its part in the rhythm of existence. A heartbeat, after all, was only alive when it carried both rise and fall, expansion and contraction.

She did not cry, but she bowed her head and silently prayed for all who had ever experienced the unimaginable pain of losing a child. It was a loss so profound that even those who had never borne a child could feel its echoes. The grief was unfathomable, but compassion could bridge that gap. In a world full of unseen battles, silent struggles, and hidden demons, comfort was the least that one could offer. And sometimes, it was everything.

Rose lifted her eyes to Anant, a newfound determination flickering within them. "We don't know the battles others fight," she whispered, "but we can make sure no one fights them alone."

The room, infused with the soft glow of candlelight, seemed warmer. The shadows on the walls no longer loomed but danced with a quiet understanding. Life was not just a collection of moments; it was a shared journey of strength, pain, hope, and love. And in that moment, Rose knew that while sorrow was inevitable, so too was the strength that followed it.

With every experience Aara endured, Rose found herself learning invaluable lessons for the days ahead. Anant's teachings echoed in her mind; each moment in life, whether joyous, or painful, serves to shape, and prepare one for future trials. Taking this to heart, Rose began to write regularly in her gratitude journal, grounding herself in reflection, and growth.

At work, Rose's recent promotion to senior editor brought new responsibilities and a new assistant, Aathya. Just 19 and balancing distant learning with her job, Aathya was a quiet, diligent presence. Her curly hair was always tied in a tight bun, and her large, dark eyes seemed perpetually wary, flinching at unexpected noises. Rose sensed that Aathya carried a hidden weight but chose not to pry. Trust, she knew, had to be earned with patience.

As days passed, Aathya grew more comfortable handling tasks and trusting Rose, but her hesitance to double-check or ask questions often meant that miscommunications led to wasted effort. Meanwhile, Aara's teachings within *Anant* resonated through Rose. Unbeknownst to Rose, the spells, and practices Aara documented were meant for her, as Aara and Vaani foresaw that Rose would be born from the culmination of their lives' energy and sacrifice. She was the child Aara lost, the essence of their dedication and love reborn.

One day, as Rose entered the office early, she found Aathya sobbing quietly at her desk. The girl, startled by Rose's unexpected arrival, quickly wiped her tears, and fled to the washroom. Rose waited, and when Aathya returned, she approached without questions, simply placing a comforting hand on her shoulder. Suddenly, Rose's vision blurred, and she was transported to a scene unfolding like a film before her eyes: a young child cowering as her mother was beaten mercilessly by two men and an old woman, who screamed insults without pause.

Rose recoiled, the vision shattering as she pulled her hand back, eyes wide with shock. "Aathya... was that you as a child? Who was that woman?" Rose asked, unable to mask her concern. Aathya's eyes filled with fear and confusion, and without a word, she hurried from the room.

After lunch, Aathya returned, hesitated at Rose's desk, then spoke. "Could we take a walk, please?" Rose nodded, telling the Chief Editor they'd investigate a rumoured mall development nearby and return later. Outside, the crisp air buzzed with unspoken tension as they found a quiet café. There, Aathya's voice trembled as she apologized for her earlier behaviour and admitted how odd it felt after Rose's touch, as though an unbearable weight was being lifted.

She revealed the painful truth: the child in the vision was indeed her. Her mother had been beaten to death after confronting Aathya's father about the years of abuse inflicted on Aathya by her uncle. The cruelty had been a constant shadow in their home, one that had scarred Aathya both physically and emotionally. Aathya confessed that her mother, in her failure to protect her, had sacrificed not only her own safety but also her voice. She had allowed her child to grow up believing that such abuses were inevitable, and that having no voice of her own was a curse too difficult to escape. Aathya had once blamed her mother for not speaking out sooner when she herself had endured years of sexual abuse at the hands of her paternal uncle. She felt betrayed by the silence, accusing her mother of failing to protect her.

But her mother had understood the weight of her failure, and despite the risks, decided to confront the family, even if it meant her own destruction. Her only desire was to ensure her daughter's safety and to stop the abuse that no one, least of all her child, deserved. Upon hearing this confrontation, Aathya's father, unable to confront his own failure to protect his daughter, turned his rage on her mother. With a twisted mindset, he blamed her for "ruining" the girl, accusing her of making Aathya so "characterless" that she faced such consequences. The heated argument spiralled out of control, and in an explosion of rage, the men who believed in physical dominance as the solution to all problems savagely beat Aathya's mother in front of her. The sight haunted Aathya for years, leaving her to grapple with the unbearable guilt of believing that she had somehow been the cause of her mother's death, the reason for her mother's tragic end.

Hearing this, Rose's heart ached with sorrow and fury. She remembered Aara's teachings on absorbing pain for others and granting them the strength to move forward. "It ends here, Aathya," Rose said softly, taking the young woman's hands. "Trust me." She closed her eyes, repeating the ancient chants she had learned from Anant. Rose felt a heavy, searing pain seep into her heart as Aathya's torment transferred to her, leaving the girl with cheeks flushed with warmth and hope for the first time in years.

Tears of relief welled in Aathya's eyes as an unfamiliar peace settled over her. She whispered, "I don't know what you did, but... I feel free." Rose smiled faintly, urging Aathya to return to the office and excuse her absence for the day.

The walk home was gruelling; pain weighed down each step until Rose reached her door. Collapsing near her study chair, she whispered, "Anant, help me. I wasn't prepared for this." The mystical book pulsed with light as wind rustled the trees outside, and Rose watched in awe as the veins in her hands glowed blue, the light dispersing from her fingertips. She recited Aara's spells of recovery until exhaustion overtook her. Pulling a blanket from the sofa, Rose curled up on the rug, surrendering to sleep as the room hummed softly with the remnants of magic and resolve.

Forgiveness is not only for others but also for oneself. It's a journey one takes to heal. Sometimes, we feel compelled to forget before we fully forgive, either the wrongdoer, or ourselves for allowing it to happen. But healing is not just about letting go; it's about growth. To truly heal, one must embrace the lessons learned from the experience, no matter how painful. Only then can we move forward. Rose, after her encounter with Aathya, understood this deeply. It was essential to forgive those who had hurt and disappointed her, not just for their sake, but also for her own peace and growth.

The next day, Anant spoke to Rose about forgiveness in a way that resonated deeply within her. He explained that healing comes not just from letting go of anger or resentment, but from seeing the bigger picture of life. He told her, "Sometimes, wrong, and hurtful things happen, but it is our choice to learn from them and grow. You cannot live fully in the present if you are still bound to the past. To heal, you must release the hurt and take the lessons with you, so that you move forward and create a better future."

Anant's words echoed in Rose's heart. She had taken the first step by being there for Aathya, by sharing her sorrow, and allowing her to feel less alone. Rose silently prayed for Aathya's mother to attain peace and for her father to face the consequences of his actions. She knew that forgiveness didn't absolve the wrongdoer but was a gift to oneself—to free one's soul from the weight of bitterness and resentment.

In the days that followed, Aathya shared a surprising revelation with Rose. Her father, after years of denial, and anger, had a change of heart. He confessed to his sins, turning himself in to the police, admitting his guilt. He was charged with murder and sentenced accordingly. Before ending the call, he apologized to Aathya, asking for forgiveness. Aathya was silent, unsure how to respond.

Rose, with a quiet compassion, told her, "It's your time to heal now, Aathya. Forgiveness may seem impossible, but it's the key to freeing yourself from the past. By forgiving, you would help your mother's soul find peace and, in turn, you begin to live a life free from fear and silence. Your future is waiting for you, and you must live it without the shadows of the past holding you back."

Aathya took her advice to heart. She continued working for a few more months before sharing with Rose that she had decided to join college full-time. There was a twist of fate that allowed her to do so. Her fees had been paid in full by an anonymous benefactor. Aathya expressed her gratitude to the "faceless soul" who had allowed her to live an everyday student life. Rose, with a knowing smile, realized the benefactor's identity. It had been the Editor-in-Chief, whose generosity, and kindness had been sparked by her own plea on Aathya's behalf.

Every year, the Chief would choose an act of kindness, and this year, with Rose's help, it had been Aathya, a young woman with a bright future, deserving a chance at a better tomorrow. Rose felt a deep sense of fulfilment, knowing that she had played a part in changing Aathya's life, guiding her towards healing, and the life she deserved.

Ramanuj Ray was the Editor-in-Chief running *The Daily Times Magazine* in the city. A towering figure in his sixties, he was a respected man in the community, known for his unwavering righteousness and his role as a "faceless messiah" to those less fortunate. His acts of kindness were legendary. Tales of his generosity circulated throughout the town. People spoke of him with admiration, grateful for the many lives he had touched through his philanthropic deeds. Despite his stature, there was an undeniable humility about him, a quiet strength that commanded respect.

Mr. Ray had a beautiful wife, Naazuk, an artist who poured her soul into painting. Yet, despite their love, and unwavering efforts, the couple had never been blessed with a child of their own. Destiny had been cruel, denying them the joy of parenthood. But rather than succumbing to sorrow, they had embraced the children of the town as their own. They channelled their love into the community, often supporting the less fortunate and ensuring that the future of the town's children was bright. They became pillars of hope, and Rose admired them deeply for their kindness and generosity.

After Mr. Ray's extraordinary act of kindness in ensuring Aathya's future was secure, Rose's respect for him grew even further. She couldn't help but feel a deep gratitude towards the couple, and in her own small way, she tried to show her appreciation. Rose would bake muffins and tea cakes for the Rays, bringing them to their home as a token of thanks. More than that, she made sure to visit them regularly, checking in on them as they had done for so many others over the years.

But Rose's visits had another layer to them. Whenever she stepped into their home, she couldn't help but notice the paintings that adorned the walls, forest scenes that seemed both familiar and strange, as if they belonged to a place she had never been but somehow knew. The forests in Naazuk's paintings were full of mystery and an eerie, yet serene beauty. Rose was drawn to them, sensing something beyond the canvas, an unspoken connection between her and the forests that seemed to call out to her.

For Naazuk Ray, Rose's appreciation of her paintings ignited something deep within her. For years, the empty silence of her home had been something they both had silently accepted, a part of their lives that they had learned to live with. But Rose's presence brought something different. Naazuk began to feel alive again, and with it, her art began to take on new energy. It was as though Rose's admiration awakened something within her, compelling her to paint with a renewed urgency.

Naazuk felt a strange pull to paint the forests, not just as they were, but as they seemed to call out to her, unknown forests, yet somehow familiar. The more she painted, the stronger the feeling became, as if the forests were reaching out to her, asking for something. It was as though they were calling Rose, and Naazuk had become their messenger, the conduit through which their message would be delivered.

With this newfound purpose, Naazuk painted with a vigour she hadn't felt in years. Each stroke seemed to connect her more deeply to the forest and to Rose. The paintings became a bridge between worlds, and Naazuk felt compelled to convey the messages hidden within them. For the first time in her life, she painted not just to express herself, but to fulfil a deeper calling; one that would bring Rose closer to a hidden truth.

Rose shared with Anant her growing connection with the Rays and how Naazuk's paintings resonated deeply within her, touching a place she hadn't fully understood. Anant listened intently, his gaze reflecting a knowing calm. "It's the nature of the forests," he said, "and your calling. The trees and soil are reaching out to you, just as they did to Aara. In the rush and noise of city life, we have lost our tether to the natural world, the part of us that aches to reconnect." He paused, letting the weight of his words settle over them. "To move closer to your true self, Rose, you must walk among the trees, chant the spells you've learned, and allow the forest to answer. And take Naazuk with you, she too, needs to hear the whispers of the woods."

Rose nodded, understanding that the journey ahead was both inward and outward. There was a hidden message, a puzzle that only she could decipher. Her path was becoming clearer, and she was ready to follow it.

When Rose invited Naazuk to join her for evening walks, Naazuk's eyes lit up with an unexpected joy. It had been years since she had stepped out of her house for something as simple as a walk. The once vibrant artist had become a recluse, burdened by unspoken guilt, and a longing that had festered over time. Rose offered, "Why don't we take a walk before dinner? It'll be good for both of us to breathe in the fresh air." Naazuk agreed, feeling an inexplicable pull in her heart.

With each walk, something in Naazuk began to shift. At first, she was tentative, feeling the weight of her years pressing down on her. But every time Rose extended her hand to help her over a rough patch or to guide her along, she felt a spark—small but undeniable. Often, she would notice slight tremors in Rose, subtle jerks that made her pause and ask, "Are you alright?" Rose would always smile and nod, but Naazuk sensed that these moments meant something more.

It was on their fifth evening walk that Naazuk finally asked, "Rose, is there something you wish to tell me? I see it in your eyes." Rose looked at her, eyes unwavering, and said, "There's a shadow in your heart, a resentment that keeps you from finding peace. You've carried it for so long, but why? You and Ramanuj have done so much good, shown so much love. Why does this bitterness remain?"

Naazuk stood still, the question catching her off guard. But it was Rose standing before her, and somehow that made it easier. Lowering her defences, Naazuk began to speak. "Rose, everyone in town knows us, knows how Ramanuj, and I have always been seen as pillars of kindness. But there's a part of our story that no one knows. When I first met Ramanuj, I was struck by his boundless kindness and humility. We were so happy, filled with dreams of a life full of love. But when it became clear that we couldn't have children, something changed."

Naazuk's voice trembled as she continued, "I knew the reason. A medical issue my doctor had confided in me. But I couldn't bear to tell Ramanuj. He blamed himself, thinking he was the reason we couldn't have children. He took it upon himself to shield me, to take on the whispers and blame of others. He said that we were enough, that perhaps destiny had a different plan for us. But deep down, I knew that he knew the truth. His silent sacrifice only deepened my guilt. I wanted to confess, to thank him for his unwavering love, but I was too ashamed, too scared.

Over the years, that silence has turned to resentment. I resented myself for not having the courage to speak, and I resented him for loving me so wholly, so selflessly."

Tears welled up in Naazuk's eyes as she whispered, "I became bitter, withdrawing into myself, unable to bear the weight of my own silence. Ramanuj never faltered. He brought me canvases, brushes, and anything to help me find peace. And painting became my only solace."

Rose listened, her heart aching with the shared burden. She guided Naazuk to a bench and gently asked her to close her eyes. Placing her hand on Naazuk's forehead, Rose began to chant, her voice steady, and soft. "You are being set free. Fate cannot be fought but must be embraced. What you create next is yours to choose. You are the weaver of your destiny, and blessed are those who find true companions on their journey. Ramanuj deserves the love he has given you, and you deserve the love you have received. Your paintings are your legacy, a gift to the world. Let them bring light and inspiration to those seeking hope."

As the words settled, a warm glow seemed to envelop Naazuk. Her face softened, and a breath she hadn't realized she'd been holding released in a long, cleansing sigh. For the first time in years, peace touched her heart.

The evening melted away as they walked back, and Rose felt an inner calm she hadn't known before. When she returned to her apartment, she found Anant waiting, glowing softly with a pink light—a sign that they had both taken another step on their shared path.

The next day, when Rose arrived at the Rays' residence, Naazuk greeted her with a warm smile but an apologetic tone. "Rose, I hope you don't mind, but today I'd like to take Ramanuj for a walk. There's something we need to discuss." Understanding immediately, Rose's eyes softened, and she nodded, returning Naazuk's smile.

Left to her own thoughts, Rose decided to take a solitary walk to the woods. As she strolled, an idea surfaced; it was the perfect day to bring Anant along. Without delay, she turned, and hurried back to her apartment.

Much to her shock, there seemed to be flares of yellow and orange moving inside. "Fire," Rose whispered, her heart lurching in her chest.

Chapter 4

It took forty horrifying minutes for the firefighters to douse the fire, sand the smouldering furniture, and finally calm the place down. When the police completed their preliminary investigation, it appeared to be from an unknown source. Still, there was no doubt that it was intentional and not an accident, as the whole place was shattered & turned upside down before setting the fire to the pile of things thrown in the centre. The fire had been set deliberately, with a precision that spoke of an intent far more sinister than mere destruction. It targeted her apartment alone, sparing the rest of the building but reducing her home to ashes.

Rose's mind raced as she sat on the footpath, knees pulled up, trembling with shock. The questions roared in her head like the dying embers of the fire: Who could have done this? Why? The air around her was heavy with smoke and the acrid scent of charred memories. An officer approached her, his face a blend of professional detachment and concern. "We've checked the area, and there's no sign of anyone suspicious or unfamiliar. For your own safety, it would be wise for you to find somewhere else to stay tonight," he advised, his voice devoid of comfort.

The first thought that pierced through Rose's stunned silence was Anant. Panic surged through her veins. "Can I go inside for a moment?" she asked, her voice wavering. The officer hesitated but nodded, understanding her desperation. Perhaps there was something only she could find, something their eyes had missed.

She stepped into what remained of her apartment, smoke,

and the scent of scorched paper stinging her nose and eyes. Ash and soot covered everything; the once-familiar space was now an alien wasteland. Her favourite books had been reduced to blackened piles, mere ghosts of the stories they once held. The blankets, now singed, and brittle, lay scattered across the floor like discarded shrouds.

With a heart clenched in fear, Rose pushed through the rubble, her gaze frantically searching. The sight of her beloved books, torn, and thrown in anger, deepened the ache in her chest. A sudden dread gripped her as she thought of Anant. What if it had suffered the same fate? She began to toss the remnants of her life aside, her hands blackened with soot, her sobs wracking her body. "Anant, where are you? Please… please call out to me," she whispered through the lump in her throat, tears carving streaks down her sooty cheeks.

A faint glimmer of pink broke through the haze, a gentle pulse of light from beneath the bed. It was Anant, its mystical glow unwavering in the face of destruction. Relief flooded her as she dropped to her knees and reached under the bed, clutching the book to her chest as if it were life itself. Whoever had set this blaze had deemed it useless, unable to read its cryptic language, and in frustration had cast it aside. A small, grim smile touched Rose's lips as she wiped her face, smudging the black further. "Simpletons," she muttered as she hugged Anant tighter.

The apartment offered nothing more but the painful echo of loss. With Anant safely in her grasp, Rose stepped out into the cool night, her heart still pounding with the residue of fear and disbelief.

"Where to go, Anant? Where do we go now?" she whispered, her voice breaking. She glanced at the book, half-hoping for an answer, half-afraid of what it might say. "Did you see the intruder's face? Tell me later, but guide me now. We need to find a place where whoever did this cannot reach us."

Anant's light flickered gently, as if nodding in agreement. It communicated a reassuring message: among all the places she knew, the Rays' residence would be the safest haven for the night. Without another moment's hesitation, Rose clutched Anant close, and started down the dimly lit street, leaving behind the smouldering remnants of her past.

As soon as the officers were informed of her temporary whereabouts, and with Ramanuj Ray himself reassuring them that Rose would be staying under his roof, the priority shifted to unravelling the mystery as swiftly as possible. The urgency in the air was palpable, each person bound by a shared determination to bring clarity to this harrowing event.

Rose felt a wave of relief wash over her as she recalled the phone call to Mr. Ray during her tense journey. Without hesitation or questions, he had told her not to stop anywhere but to come straight to their home. She knew Ramanuj was not just any man. He was a respected senior journalist, deeply connected in circles where whispers of the world travelled fast. It was likely that he had already heard of the fire before her call, but the warmth in his voice told her that this was not just another story for him. When the door swung open, he stood there, eyes heavy with concern. He pulled her into a gentle, reassuring half-hug, guiding her inside with quiet strength.

"Naazuk!" he called out, his voice steady but laced with worry. "Rose is here. Everything ready?"

Naazuk appeared at the top of the stairs, her expression softening as she saw Rose. In a heartbeat, she was by her side, embracing her tightly as though they had shared a bond spanning lifetimes. The empathy etched into Naazuk's features made it clear she understood the storm of emotions tearing through Rose's chest, the shock, the fear, the aching disbelief. "We've set up the guest room for you," Naazuk said softly, her voice a soothing balm. "Stay as long as you need. There's no rush, Rose."

Tears welled up in Rose's eyes, spilling over as she felt the full weight of their kindness. This wasn't just shelter; it was a lifeline in her time of need. The walls around her heart, built brick by brick during a lonely childhood, trembled, and cracked. How could these people, not even bound to her by blood, be so open, so unwavering in their generosity?

"Go wash up, get the dust and ash off your face," Naazuk insisted, her eyes glistening with both worry and resolve. "You must eat something tonight. You need your strength back. This isn't the time to feel small or powerless." Rose nodded, though her limbs felt as though they were carved from stone. Her mind raced with the weight of the truth: someone had done this to her, deliberately. The questions gnawed at her: who, why, how? She needed to find the answers, not just to understand but also to protect herself from whatever darkness had come for her.

Ramanuj watched her with a quiet, measured gaze, the flicker of concern in his eyes betraying the thoughts he kept to himself. He knew the fight ahead would be heavy, and Rose would need all the courage she could muster. He reached out, placing a firm but gentle hand on her head, a gesture of solidarity. "Take your time, Rose. When you're ready, we'll be waiting for you downstairs," he said, his voice low, and comforting.

Rose took a deep breath, feeling the beginnings of strength return as she turned towards the stairs. She had a safe place, at least for now. And with that, she could start piecing together the shattered fragments of her life.

Rose stepped into a warm bath, letting the heat seep into her bones and ease the chill that had settled deep within her. The steam curled around her, blurring the harsh edges of the day and calming the storm in her mind. The water felt like a protective shield, and for the first time since the fire, she allowed herself a moment to breathe. The silence, punctuated by the soft lapping of water, wrapped around her like a balm.

When she emerged, her skin flushed, and her heart a fraction steadier, she noticed the thoughtful arrangements that Naazuk had made. A few items of clothing were neatly folded in the closet, a silent acknowledgement that Rose had come empty-handed. But it was more than just clothes. There were undergarments, toiletries, soap, shampoo, a delicate bottle of perfume, and even a pair of soft slippers. The sheer attentiveness behind these gestures made Rose's chest tighten with emotion. Naazuk had anticipated her needs with such care, filling in the gaps without question or expectation.

Rose's thoughts wandered as she dressed in a comfortable T-shirt and pyjama set, slipping her feet into the warm slippers. She felt the weight of gratitude press against her, mingled with an ache that never quite left her heart. How cruel fate could be, she mused, for a woman who had grown up yearning for a family like this, warm, attentive, safe. And yet, here were the Rays, who embodied everything she had ever longed for but lacked the one thing they seemed to yearn for most: a child to share their legacy, to carry their kindness into future generations.

Before she left the room, Rose paused. Her eyes caught the edge of Anant, peeking out from under the pillow where she had placed him earlier. She reached out, fingers brushing the worn cover with a touch that was both tender and fierce. She vowed, in that quiet space, that she would never leave him vulnerable again.

Anant was more than a book; he was her confidant, her guide, and now more than ever, she needed him to stay safe. With a deep breath, she clutched him close, feeling a pulse of reassurance that only he could give.

Determined, Rose stepped out into the hallway, leaving behind the echo of water droplets and the weight of ashes, ready to face whatever lay ahead with a newfound resolve.

As Rose stepped into the dining room, she paused at the threshold, unnoticed. Ramanuj sat at the table, his expression attentive yet shadowed with concern, while Naazuk leaned slightly towards him, speaking in soft, measured tones. It wasn't just a conversation; it was an exchange filled with unspoken trust and mutual understanding. The way they looked at each other, deeply listening, reminded Rose of a bond she had longed for but never quite found. It stirred something fragile within her, a mixture of yearning, and gratitude.

A wave of warmth washed over her, bittersweet, and sudden. Without thinking, she closed her eyes, recalling the ancient words Aara had once shared. It was during a tender moment when Aara blessed her sister and brother-in-law, imparting a spell meant to fortify their love and help them withstand life's storms together. Rose whispered the chant under her breath, the syllables dancing like a soft breeze over her lips. It was a simple act, almost instinctive, yet it filled the room with an invisible thread of hope and protection.

"Come, Rose, sit with us," Naazuk called, her voice warm, and inviting as she pulled out the chair beside her. Rose took a breath, steadying herself before walking over and settling into the seat. The table was modestly set with a bowl of fresh salad, a dish of simple pasta, and empty glasses that hinted at the promise of wine, something Rose realized she desperately needed tonight.

Dinner passed in an unusual silence, heavy with unasked questions. The tragedy that had upended Rose's life loomed unspoken between them, an uninvited guest that none dared to acknowledge. The tension was palpable, yet there was a comforting quiet in the way no one forced her to speak. They ate, sharing a meal that offered more solace than words could.

When the plates were cleared, Rose stood up to help Ramanuj tidy up the table and stack the dishes in the kitchen. It was an almost sacred act of normalcy, a brief respite from the storms of uncertainty. Meanwhile, Naazuk's gentle nature shone through as she poured wine into their glasses, her eyes crinkling with a soft smile. "I think you'll like this one. Ramanuj brought it back from overseas a few years ago when he went for research."

With a nod, Naazuk handed out the glasses, and Rose accepted hers with a quiet thank you. She took a small sip, savouring the sharp sweetness before moving to the window. The cool night air swept in, brushing her face with a crispness that cleared her mind. Unconsciously, she whispered into the breeze, "Was it a threat?"

The response came in a whisper only the trees could send, a rustle that seemed almost like a word: "Yes."

A shiver ran down her spine as she stared out into the darkness, her pulse quickening. Had she truly heard it, or was exhaustion, and fear playing tricks on her? The wine in her glass caught her eye, glistening with tiny, swirling flecks of red that hadn't been there moments ago. Her chest tightened as the realization set in, the answer as clear as the night sky: He had found her. He was here, in the city, seeking her out.

Rose's fingers tightened around the glass as she fought to steady her breathing. The haven she had found now trembled on the edge of a storm she thought she'd left behind.

The next morning, Rose slipped into the borrowed clothes Naazuk had thoughtfully laid out for her. They fit her perfectly, as though they had been tailored for her, but they were still strange to her skin, foreign in a way that only clothes that weren't your own could be. She could feel their warmth, the kindness stitched into them, but it didn't stop the cold unease that clung to her chest. With a soft thank you to Naazuk, she left for the office with Ramanuj, the weight of the day ahead pressing down on her.

A few minutes into the drive, unable to shake the unease gnawing at him, Ramanuj broke the silence. "Are you sure you want to go to the office today, Rose? You could stay home, rest, and think things through with Naazuk."

Rose paused. The offer to stay back was kind, but her mind was already too chaotic. The notion of taking time off felt like an indulgence she couldn't afford. She needed something to distract her, something to occupy the space where her fear festered. "I need to be at work, Ramanuj. I need the distraction, at least until I can find a way to process this... this threat."

The admission tumbled out before she could stop it, raw, and vulnerable. The weight of her own words startled her, and for a moment, she dared to glance at Ramanuj, catching the concern deepening in his eyes. She realized that Ramanuj and Naazuk were actually the only ones she could trust. They were the ones she could rely on in a world that felt suddenly very dangerous.

Her eyes lowered, her hands clenching at her sides as the full weight of her own confession settled in. The words had left her thoughts and taken the form of a naked truth. It was time, she realized, to stop running from her past and face what was right in front of her.

With a deep, steadying breath, Rose spoke again, her voice quieter this time but resolute. She began to tell him everything.

The story of her childhood, of being an only child to a mother who sacrificed her dreams to support a husband who was never there. Her father, absent in both body, and heart, had been consumed by endless responsibilities to his family, leaving Rose, and her mother to live their lives in service to others, their needs ignored, and their voices unheard. She described the suffocating loneliness she had always felt, trapped in a house that was supposed to be home but never felt like it.

Then came the pain of losing her mother, an ache that no child should ever experience, let alone one left alone with a father who hadn't even been there to grieve. The darkness of those days stretched on, and the horror of it all took shape with her words. She spoke of her desire to escape, her longing to be free, and how it led her to college, far away, where she could build a life for herself, even if it meant being alone.

But her words faltered as she recalled the man who had once shown her kindness, only to become the source of her deepest wounds, the man who had turned from protector to predator, who had beaten her into silence. Rose's voice quivered as she recounted those months of terror, the nights spent beside him, his hands brutal, and unyielding. She spoke of the dread she had felt, knowing that he was the only person outside her family who cared enough to drag her into a life of captivity. He had wanted to marry her, drag her into his home, where she would be trapped forever.

With each word, Rose's heart cracked a little more. She hadn't shared this part of herself with anyone before, not in such detail, not with this kind of raw honesty. Her breath hitched as she spoke of her eventual escape, of running away in the dead of night, leaving behind everything she knew, and going into the unknown.

Ramanuj sat in silence, his face stricken with an emotion he couldn't name. He felt gutted hearing Rose's confession, the weight of her pain sinking into his chest like a stone. He hadn't known the extent of what she'd been through. How much she'd suffered; how many years of fear and abuse had been etched into her soul. It sickened him to think of the man who had caused her so much pain.

And yet, as Rose finished speaking, a dreadful realization began to gnaw at him. The person she had spoken of, the man who had hurt her, was likely the same one who had tracked her down. The thought sent a chill through him. How could anyone carry such rage for so long, for years, only to find the person they'd once tormented, and the first thing they did was to burn down everything she had built to ash? Ramanuj clenched his fists, a wave of anger, and helplessness rising in him.

He couldn't believe what he was hearing. Rose, the woman who had lived through so much, now had to face this new horror. He only wished there was something more he could do to shield her from the monster who had followed her into the present.

"We need to report this to the police, Rose. They need to hear it from you—straight from the source. That way, there'll be no doubt. It's him, isn't it?" Ramanuj's voice was firm, yet a hint of worry laced his words as he reached for his notepad. His gaze met Rose's, steady, and insistent. "What was his name again?" he asked, poised to write it down.

The question made Rose's heart stop for a beat. She felt a shiver ripple through her, the kind that raised the fine hairs at the back of her neck. For so many years, she had avoided speaking his name aloud, as if the act itself would breathe life into the monster from her past. The old saying whispered in her mind: Speak of the devil and he shall appear. She had kept that part of her history buried, tucked away in the dark corners where it felt unreal, almost like a shadow that could only haunt her in memory. But now, it was creeping back into her present, tangible, and threatening.

With a tremor in her voice and a look that spoke of a thousand fears, Rose whispered, "His name is Tapas Amin." The words felt foreign on her tongue, like shards of glass. The name carried the weight of every bruised moment; every breathless hour spent in terror. She swallowed hard. "He was two years older than me. He must be around twenty-eight now."

Ramanuj noted the name, but his eyes never left her face, searching for some way to comfort her without words. Rose's mind flooded with images she had long fought to erase. Tapas's tall frame looming over her, the dark brown hair that shone almost black in the moonlight, like the leaves of an ancient, shadowed tree. His eyes, sharp, and cold, mirroring the calculating mind behind them. Born into wealth and privilege, he had grown up as the spoiled only son of powerful landowners, surrounded by affluence that had taught him the world was his to take and control.

"If he's in town," she said, her voice quivering as realization dawned, "then he must already know where I work, which route I take, and maybe, where I am right now. He always knew how to track me, like he had an instinct for it." The confession pressed heavily into her chest, making it hard to breathe.

She admitted to Ramanuj what she had never voiced before, even to herself. "For years, I convinced myself that he had moved on, that what we had, or what he thought we had, was just a dark chapter that faded with time. I thought running away was enough, that my silence was enough. But I see now that I was wrong." Her eyes shimmered with a deep, haunted fear, and she looked down, twisting her hands together. "To think he's been holding onto that rage all this time… It's terrifying. He's here to remind me that peace is not mine to have. That I am accountable for daring to leave, for thinking I could ever escape him."

The space seemed to shrink around her, heavy with the weight of her words. Ramanuj, usually composed, felt a surge of protective anger rise in him. How could one man's cruelty linger on for so long, festering into a force that would drive him to find her after all these years? He reached out and gently placed a hand on Rose's shoulder, his eyes filled with resolve. "We'll get through this," he said softly, though inside, he was already calculating their next steps to keep her safe.

Ramanuj changed route and headed for the police station. The ride thereafter was cold and silent. The city outside passed by in a blur, its usual hustle-bustle muted beneath the weight of Rose's thoughts. Relaying all the information bare before the police and describing the man brought a mixture of emotions. Regret gnawed at her for not recognizing the signs earlier and failing to protect herself. But there was also an unfamiliar sense of calm—at least now, she realized, she was strong enough to ask for help.

Ramanuj glanced at her with a soft, reassuring nod, a silent reminder that she wasn't alone anymore. She had people by her side, ready to help her navigate this storm.

Reaching the car, Rose's legs felt weak. "I think you're right, Ramanuj," she said as they stood by the kerb. "Resting at home today might be best. After confessing so much, to you, to the police… It's like I need to piece myself back together."

Talking had stripped the power from her anxieties. The shadowy figures of her memories seemed less ominous now, since they'd been pulled into the light. Speaking out loud had dulled their sharp edges, softened their grip on her mind. Talking takes away a worry's power to control you, she realized. It was something she had known in theory but now she understood deeply, with every breath.

Taking a deep breath, she bid goodbye to Ramanuj, who squeezed her shoulder before heading to work. The parting left her standing alone, yet not lonely. Each step back towards the Rays' home felt different, lighter.

Anant, she told herself, could help her. The mystical guide had seen the potential in her long before she dared to see it in herself. Until yesterday, she had clung to scepticism, finding it easier to dismiss the power within than face it. But now, with the remnants of her fear laid bare and no alternative but to draw strength from within, she knew she needed to believe. Believing wasn't just a choice; it was survival.

Rose gently knocked on the door; the warmth of the Ray household wrapped around her like a much-needed refuge. Opening the door, Naazuk seemed pleased to see Rose had changed her mind and come back home.

"You're back, and just in time," Naazuk said, her voice like balm on Rose's ailing heart. "I was just brewing some tea. Would you care for some? After a few seconds, she added, "We can have it in the garden at the back, if you like."

Rose managed a small, apologetic smile. "Thank you, Naazuk. If you don't mind, I think I'll rest for a bit. Would it be okay if I go to the guest room?" she asked, her eyes pleading.

"Of course," Naazuk replied, placing a hand lightly on Rose's arm. "I'll be in the study if you need anything. Just come down or call out, okay?"

Rose followed Naazuk to the kitchen, where there was peace in the silence that lingered in their home. How beautiful it was to have the opportunity to build a home with someone you love, where both of you bring elements that appeal to you, like pieces of a puzzle, each fitting together to create something perfect as a whole. The walls were lined with books and paintings, many of which Naazuk had made over the years, each piece reflecting something about Naazuk and Ramanuj's union.

Naazuk poured the hot, honey coloured tea into a tiny porcelain cup with green petals on its rim and handed it to Rose.

Rose nodded in thanks and took a couple of steps back, turning. She could feel the warmth of Naazuk's presence seeping into her, soothing the edges of her exhaustion. How grateful she was to have found them. Turning her back towards the kitchen, she walked back to the lobby and climbed the stairs, chanting the protective spell she had learned from Aara. Until now, she had used it only for those she cared about, but this time, it was for herself.

When she entered her room, Anant seemed to be waiting for her, resting quietly under the pillow where she had hidden him the night before. The sight of it brought a flicker of solace. She closed the door behind her, letting out a sigh that felt as if it had been lodged in her chest for years. Setting the cup of tea down, she walked over and hugged the book tightly, drawing strength from the familiar touch and the steady pulse of warmth that seemed to emanate from it.

She took a sip of the tea, allowing it to ease her mind. Settling into the reading chair by the window and absorbing the warm golden rays spreading across her face, Rose opened Anant. The pages awakened, with images of leaves rustling and swirling in the breeze from the open window, as if the book was once more coming alive in her hands. The pictures stirred to life, resuming the tale where she had left off. There was Aara, cradled in Aameen's arms amidst the ruins, the aftermath of chaos etched on both their faces. The scene tugged at Rose's heart, echoing her own turmoil. Rose turned the page to see what happened next.

When Aara woke up and adjusted her eyes to the sunlight streaming through the window, she saw Aameen carefully placing fresh wild yellow flowers into the vase nearby. He remembers, she thought. Aara had only mentioned once in passing her fascination with wildflowers, especially yellow ones, the kind that grew on trails not meant to be tread upon. The thought that Aameen had taken the trouble to gather them for her warmed her heart.

Aameen's movements were swift, as if he were in a hurry to fix the place, relying on the Dai's reassurance that Aara would regain consciousness any day now. He wanted to ensure the room was ready when Aara awoke. He wanted her to feel at home and safe. Aameen had entrusted the Dai with overseeing Aara's well-being. Caring for her while she lay helpless was as important to him as protecting her.

The villagers held a deep reverence for Aara, believing that she was a rare and powerful deity they had always prayed to, the purest, and most selfless being they had ever encountered. It was this belief that made them respect Aameen's insistence on keeping the cottage under watch whenever he was away. Though Aameen spent hours by Aara's side, he still needed to find a means of livelihood. He soon discovered his artistic talents in carpentry, crafting furniture that was both unique and masterful. Each creation was a testament to the inspiration he found in Aara, who had unknowingly helped him unearth parts of himself he hadn't realized were there.

Seeing Aara awake and smiling at him with tears in her eyes, Aameen's heart swelled, and tears brimmed in his eyes too. He ushered the Dai and others out of the room and embraced Aara, his love mingling with the sorrow of their shared loss. He kissed her gently, apologizing, and vowing that she would never again have to feel so helpless as to defend herself alone. Aara, with a soft smile, reassured him that it was he she had always sought to protect, willing to sacrifice herself again if needed. Though both bore the weight of grief, they knew their bond was pure and that their love would ultimately fill the void with new life and hope.

Aameen shared how the near-tragedy had changed him. Though he once believed he was destined to wander, that day's fear had made him realize those beliefs were fleeting. What truly mattered was a happy home, with Aara safe, and by his side. He spoke about the skills he had developed, still amazed at the intricate, unique pieces his hands created, pieces that seemed fit for an auction. During her recovery, he had poured himself into building their cottage, ensuring she would have a place of her own to heal. He confessed that, though thoughts of returning to his family crossed his mind, he knew they would never fully understand or move past the loss. Their harsh words would only deepen the shadows, and Aameen was determined to protect Aara from that.

Aara felt a sense of peace knowing Aameen had found his purpose, even if it came at a heavy cost. She resolved to let grief take its natural course, to cry and mourn fully, knowing that only then would healing be possible. As she relaxed in Aameen's arms, she offered him the comfort he needed, the reassurance that she was alive, present, and with him. Together, they would face whatever lay ahead, carrying the strength of their love into each new day.

Aameen encouraged Aara to rest and regain her strength before he left for work. As soon as the cottage was empty, Aara summoned Vaani and spoke to her about the conversation they had had the previous night when she had regained consciousness after months. She wanted to reaffirm the nature of the practice she would commit her days to, but first, she needed to endure a period of solitude to regain her powers.

While Aara and Vaani discussed the details, a commotion outside caught Aara's attention. The two villagers assigned to guard Aara's cottage looked anxious. Stepping outside, Aara inquired about the noise. A pale woman in her thirties informed her that the Dai's son had fallen from a tree while playing and had tumbled down a rocky slope. He had suffered a severe blow to his head and a painfully twisted leg. The child's howls and the mother's desperate cries were audible from where Aara stood.

Aameen was working in his workshop on the outskirts of the village, unaware of the commotion. Aara, still frail but recovering, steadied herself, and asked one of the women to call the Dai and bring the child to her. The thought of the young boy in pain and the mother's anguish, especially the same woman who had tenderly cared for her, moved Aara deeply.

The Dai, upon hearing Aara's summons, did not hesitate. Trusting Aara's inexplicable aura, she rushed to comply, holding her son tightly in her arms with hope and desperation in her eyes.

Aara sat down and gently took the child in her arms. She closed her eyes, steadied her breath, and, with deliberate care, held the child's head, and then his leg, which she gently straightened while chanting words that came from deep within. Her chanting was so intense that no one could hear her words; they could only see tears streaming from her eyes and the anxiety on her face. Within minutes, the boy gasped once, and then fell silent, slipping into a deep, calm sleep. Aara opened her eyes and looked at the boy's mother.

"He's resting, Dai *Ma*," Aara said softly. "He will be well in a day or two. There will be some soreness in his leg, but that too will pass."

The mother bent to touch Aara's feet, thanking her between sobs. Aara held her by the shoulders. "Please, don't thank me. You were there for my family, and I am forever grateful." She lifted the Dai from the floor, where she had fallen in gratitude, and urged her to go home.

The villagers gathered at the doorway stood transfixed, their wide eyes filled with awe and disbelief. It was as if they had witnessed a miracle. Slowly, they dispersed, whispering with wonder. One of the men carried the boy home under the Dai's direction, while she lingered a moment longer to hear Aara's request.

"Dai Ma, I need to observe a 13-day mourning period," Aara said, her voice steady but solemn. "I will need water from the village well and seeds from different plants to sustain myself during this time. Could you arrange this for me?"

The Dai's eyes filled with tears. "My goddess, you healed my child with your bare hands. You took away his pain and gave him peace. I will do as you ask and return with everything you need."

With that, the Dai left, determined, and in a hurry. Aara closed the door behind her and retreated to her bed.

When Aameen returned later, he found Aara stitching a black robe in the corner. Concern clouded his face as he asked why she was working when she needed rest.

Aara met his eyes and explained the 13-day mourning period, a tribute she needed to pay for their unborn child and the men who had died that dark day. She told him that being part of nature meant honouring it and seeking atonement for using her powers so violently. Mother Nature demanded repentance, regardless of intention.

"I need to do this, Aameen," she said. "To release the grief and keep my heart pure."

Aara mentally prepared for the arguments and concerns she expected Aameen to raise, but to her surprise, although he didn't fully grasp all that she felt, he agreed.

"I trust your *judgment* and the deep wisdom you carry," he said. "I respect your decision, Aara. I'll stay outside the cottage so you can do what you need to without disturbance."

With his words, a serene understanding settled over them both.

The night was silent and calm. Aara's mind was racing; she had a feeling that something lurked in the woods, keeping an eye on them. Vaani, can you hear me? Aara said in her mind.

"Yes, Aara, I am right here, and I know something is bothering you. But it's not the time to investigate. Taking care of the eyes and knowing their whereabouts can wait. Right now, keep your focus on what's more important and needs to be addressed immediately."

Aara couldn't bear it any longer and sat up to press her left foot. She used both hands and closed her eyes while sitting. Unable to hold it in any longer, tears started running down her face as her hands, with a flickering glow, warmed her aching leg.

Aameen sat up. He had been watching Aara and observing the frown and agony on her face. He couldn't understand what had happened, but he could see that Aara was deep in thought.

"Aara, what's wrong? Why do you look so pale?" Aameen asked, his face filled with worry.

Aara, already so weak, had no will to lie or hide anything from Aameen anymore. She confessed that every healing she performed came with a price. Every spell she cast to heal the person before her, brought the pain and agony of others to herself. She told him about what had happened with Dai's son and that, although she had managed to heal him, she was now too weak to remove the pain from her own body. She knew she still could, but it was taking longer than usual.

At first, Aameen couldn't understand, but seeing how Aara was holding her leg, even though there was no wound, and the tears in her eyes were enough to show she wasn't making it up. She was truly in pain.

"I don't understand. If you're not well, so weak... how did you heal the boy and absorb his pain? Why did you heal him? He could have been healed in his own time. Why did you burden yourself with more agony than what you're already going through?" Aameen said, his face turning cold as he felt anger rising.

"Calm down, Aameen. This shall pass. Hearing the cries of the little boy, I couldn't hold myself back. I couldn't turn my back on the purpose of my life. I know it isn't easy to understand, but we must be there for one another in times of need. I indeed feel gratitude and humble obligation towards Dai Ma for looking after me and you while I was unconscious, but leaving a child in pain when I know I can take it from him… how could I do that?"

Aara closed her eyes and tried again to ignite the power within her. Mother Nature, I know I am weak, but I am your child. I am still strong enough to endure this. Please give me the power to let this pain trickle down into the land I stand on.

Saying this, Aara stood straight on the floor, and Aameen, for the first time in his life, saw Aara's veins in her leg glow blue, the colour then slowly trickling down from her body into the spot where she stood. Like roots, it formed veins on the floor and began to vanish.

She took a deep sigh and sat back on the bed. After a couple of deep breaths, Aara told Aameen about herself. Her powers to protect and heal, her unbound connection with the elements of nature, and the daily prayers, and meditation she performed to show gratitude to Mother Nature for bringing her into this world. She also spoke of how she invested time in herself to strengthen her power to help those around her. Aara was about to tell Aameen about Vaani, but something held her back. It might have been too much for Aameen to comprehend, and there was no reason to frighten him or make him believe the rumours that had spread in the village about her being a witch. Sceptical, Aara wondered if, after what she had confessed and what Aameen had seen with his own eyes, he might consider her one with fearful, pleading eyes. Aara asked Aameen if he could accept her, knowing she was different from him. "Not a witch," she had to add. "Please, never call me that. Just see me as a blessed soul, someone sent to protect, and nurture humanity as much as she can." Aara tried hard not to sound odd or pretentious. She was simply a girl filled with love and care for the world around her.

Aameen did not respond immediately; he gave an awkward smile. He said, "Maybe you're right. It all seems a little hard to comprehend, but I will try to understand you and be there for you as much as I can and in whatever capacity I am needed."

Two things happened that day: firstly, for the first time, Aara spoke aloud about her purpose in life, reaffirming her belief that she could and would dedicate her life to aiding, nurturing, and helping others. Secondly, although Aameen was hopeful about understanding Aara, he felt a slight wound to his ego, thinking that Aara might never need him to protect her. She might be too self-sufficient.

Aara might have brushed this aside, but Vaani couldn't. Vaani read the look on Aameen's face and the gulp of shame that came with misunderstanding Aara's intentions. Assuming that Aara didn't really need him and recalling what had happened to her while protecting him, Aameen was hurt for the wrong reasons, but hurt nonetheless.

On the last day of fasting and penance, Vaani appeared in a pink flame before Aara and told her that Mother Nature was very pleased with her. There was something off in Vaani's voice that Aara couldn't shake. When Aara asked Vaani to share what was bothering her, Vaani sighed and spoke, "Aara, my concern lies with Aameen. I am glad you spoke to him and shared whatever you could, but him realizing the extent of your powers and abilities in such silence... and that troubled look in his eyes... I fear that a storm of misunderstanding might be brewing within him. Aara, it's time you understand that our society is built on patriarchal values. Men are raised to believe they are the providers and protectors, the saviours of those they care for. When that belief is challenged, it can strike at the very core of their identity."

Vaani sighed and continued, "Aameen, knowing that you might not need his protection, seeing how self-sufficient you are, and how you can keep everything around you protected, stands at a delicate threshold. He can either choose to see you, his companion, as an equal, or he might end up seeing this as a challenge to his pride and ingrained beliefs. For men like Aameen, the eldest son in his family, accustomed to having the right to speak, choose for himself, and make decisions while his family quietly abides, recognizing the strength, and capability of a woman can be difficult, not because of any lack of love or respect, but because of the fear that their role as protector is no longer needed. This realization, if not guided by wisdom and openness, can lead to insecurity, and conflict. That is why I want you to help Aameen see past this and understand that your strength does not diminish him or his abilities but completes the bond you share. Until then, we must tread carefully, for misunderstandings fuelled by pride lead to paths of hurt and separation, which I would never wish upon anyone, least of all you."

Aara understood well that Vaani wouldn't have shared her fears if they weren't genuinely troubling her. Their bond of sisterhood was much more than for mere guidance; they had vouched to look out for one another. Though Vaani was like Aara's inner voice, she was more adept at picking up subtle cues that Aara's human instincts often overlooked or dismissed as overthinking. Aara nodded in understanding and promised Vaani that she would do whatever was needed to protect their bond and would try to untangle the misunderstandings clouding Aameen's mind.

The dark, looming cloud, and the watchful set of eyes were another concern for Aara, which she now thought was best to confront. Aara shared with Vaani that during her prayers before the elements, she had sensed that a pair of eyes and ears had been set upon her and Aameen. The couple had drawn the attention of an old priest, one who reeked of ill will and black magic. Although Aara didn't understand the root cause of his focus, she felt an unsettling sense of jitters and fear emanating from his presence. She knew that displaying her power in a moment of rage had drawn this person closer, and for reasons unknown, he exuded an intent to harm her.

Vaani listened in silence and then agreed, "Yes, Aara, I share your concern. I asked you to focus on solitude before confronting this lurking threat because you needed to replenish your powers, as that was most important. Only when you are well from within can you protect the people you love." Vaani, validating Aara's fears, explained that this dark figure intended to harm her because her very existence challenged his power. His ego was wounded knowing that his disciples only spoke of Aara's praises since they had heard of the dark day of chaos and how, despite being a woman, Aara embodied the very deity they worshipped. How could a woman take a man's place? It was a challenge to his honour and supremacy, which Aara now had to avoid.

Vaani reminded Aara that fighting and justifying herself and her gifts was not her purpose. These powers were bestowed upon her and earned through her deeds. Yes, Aara was born with an extraordinary energy surging through her veins, but she had mastered them through her unyielding dedication. One does not become entitled without merit; it is warranted through worthiness. Aara had proven, over the years, that she was worthy of every blessing and power she held.

"Then should I fight it?" Aara asked.

"No, my child, no," Vaani replied with a comforting voice. "The future holds mysteries we are not meant to confront in the present. What the present demands is that you invest your time in practising your art and protecting and nurturing the people around you. Your concerns will find their answers when the time is right."

Saying this, Vaani bid her goodnight, and the flame subsided, leaving Aara in deep thought and with profound love in her heart.

The days that followed passed quietly and, to Aara's surprise, peacefully. Aameen tried his best to fight the insecurities that were seizing him, directing his time, and energy into carpentry and honing his craft. He began to receive bidders and purchasers from distant villages who had heard of his mastery in woodwork. Some would request to meet his wife, hoping she might have a remedy for their ailments, to which Aameen quietly obliged. Gradually, he began making excuses, and stopped bringing anyone home with him. He wanted to keep this aspect of their life separate from his personal life, knowing that his growing temper might cause discord between him and Aara. He became more mindful, which Aara embraced with the utmost love and compassion. Now and then, she allowed him to scold her or let him guide her through minor issues and misunderstandings, letting him take the lead in resolving them so that he, too, would feel compelled to nurture and protect the bond they shared.

One night, Aara and Aameen were startled awake by loud, incessant banging on their front door. With urgency, Aameen asked Aara to stay put and went to see what was happening. An old man stood there, clutching a large, brown stick that seemed to have been carved from an ancient tree, using it as his cane. His eyes, filled with desperation, pleaded as he explained that a vicious, poisonous snake had bitten his young grandson. The villagers believed it to be the snake of the devil, and no one dared to touch the boy, as it was said that anyone who came into contact with the victim of the poison would suffer a slow, painful death himself. The old man begged Aameen to ask Aara for help, for she was known far and wide as a powerful, pure soul who never turned away those in need, no matter how dire the situation.

Aara could hear the old man's pleas, but her intuition told her to wait for Aameen to come and get her, not to move until he did. Aameen, standing at the door, glanced back to see if Aara had heard and was coming. He was momentarily paralyzed with rage and doubt, wondering if Aara would go on her own without waiting for his request. When she did not appear, and the old man's cries continued, tears streaming down his face, Aameen turned back into the room and approached Aara.

"Aara, do you think you can help them?" he asked, his ego, and rage dissipating as he looked at her. Bathed in the soft glow of moonlight from the window, Aara's face was serene, pure, and full of peace, untainted by any ill will or resentment. Aameen's heart clenched as he realized the months he had spent tormented by his ego and insecurities. How could he have been so blind? This woman, before him, loved, and cared for him in ways no one else could. She had sacrificed everything for him, even when it put her own life at risk. And yet, he had responded with coldness and hurtful words, all because of his wounded pride.

A sudden rush of shame swept over him. "Aara, someone needs your help. You heard him, right?" he said, then thought, "Why didn't you go when you heard his cries? Why did you wait for me?"

Aara looked at him with calm eyes and said, "You asked me to wait, Aameen. You are my husband, but more than that, you are the love of my life. Whatever I do, whatever my purpose may be, I owe my heart, and soul to you. If you ask me to wait, I will wait, even if it takes an eternity for you to return and tell me to move."

Aameen's eyes filled with tears. "My love, we will talk later. Right now, we must go with the old man."

As they prepared to leave, a new worry flickered in Aameen's heart. He glanced at Aara, who, sensing his fear, said, "Don't worry, my love. I will be all right. But if something happens to me while I absorb the pain," (no one but Aameen knew that Aara absorbed the ailments and pains of others; to everyone else, it seemed as if the illness vanished, like magic) "remember to bring me home quickly and lay me down in the backyard on the earth. Mother Nature and the elements within me will come to my aid."

The couple, along with the old man, rushed to the west end of the village. The village seemed deserted. From afar, they could see a small cottage at the end of the road, with lanterns in the hands of the crowd, illuminating the place in a circle. When Aara and Aameen reached the cottage, they saw a young boy, no more than eight years old, lying pale, and blue on the floor. No one dared to hold him or offer him water, despite his desperate cries.

Aara felt rage building inside her. How could no one give the boy the water he was pleading for? Ignoring the warnings of those around her to be careful, Aara rushed into the cottage, poured some water into a small glass kept beside the mud pot, and hurried back to the boy. Taking him into her arms, she gently gave him water, drop by drop, sip by sip. Eventually, the boy closed his eyes and seemed to faint.

Suddenly, an unseen force made Aara close her eyes as well. It felt as if she had been transported into the child's mind, trapped in a dark room. She heard the boy's whimpering and realized that it was not an ordinary snakebite but black magic that had taken hold of him ...of her.

It was dark, but the boy's cries were loud enough for Aara to follow. Reaching for him in the darkness was Aara's immediate concern. As her eyes adjusted, she realized she was in a forest, though she had no idea where. Raising her right hand, Aara snapped her fingers, and a flame came to life on the tip of her forefinger. She caught the flame with her left hand and held it like a lamp. The forest became more visible, and Aara followed the sound of the boy, calling out to him.

She felt a cold wind whistling around her, and after a couple of calls, the wind seemed to rush towards her. Aara stood her ground and looked at the breeze as it passed, sweeping right through her. Confused by what had just happened, she suddenly heard a voice.

"You are powerful. I have gathered as much. Did you think I would be one of those fools you made vanish without even blinking? Yes, I know about them. I sent them," the man said. Over the past few weeks, there had been numerous accidents involving animals, and Aara had supported families and comforted children. The man's voice revealed that, while Aara believed she knew everything, she had missed a crucial detail: while curing those children and absorbing their pain and poison, each was laced with black magic, magic for which Aara had no remedy. Though she thought the poison had left her body, it had, in fact, lain dormant within her.

"This is the end of the road, and you've walked right into death's trap," the man continued, laughing mockingly. "You are just a woman. A silly, petty woman who thought she could make a difference with a few tricks! How naive. Everyone will soon see how you failed to save the child, and all the hope you ignited in these people and the followers you gathered will vanish. You will be left alone to die, suffering from the collective poisons within you and the pain of seeing another child lost due to your incompetence. Wouldn't that be a fitting end for you and this life you've built? Do not worry about your husband; he too, holds poison in his heart against you. He will be glad to know he no longer has to fight to maintain his dominance and respect as the man of the house, while a 'witch' was hailed as more than him in the village, a woman who turned out to be nothing but a power-hungry failure." Blowing the flame off Aara's hand, the man's laughter grew fainter and fainter, like a wind passing by, drifting away from her until silence enveloped the air once more.

Aara, stunned, couldn't comprehend, or move for a couple of seconds until it struck her. The child must be somewhere nearby, and she had to save him before thinking of herself. She pushed aside the rising heat inside her body, realizing it must be the poisons that had been dormant until now. Time was running out, and she understood the urgency of the situation. She felt almost foolish for a moment; she was surrounded by the elements, air, water, land, and fire, all within, and around her. Smiling faintly, she closed her eyes. "I summon you, wherever you are, my child.

Find your way to me... climb the wind that tugs at your shoulders and the ground that moves beneath your feet. Close your eyes and believe," Aara called out loudly, beginning to chant protective spells for the boy.

A rush of air, shaped like a bird, came whistling around Aara, and then darted into the forest to find the child. Chanting through her lips and her right hand pressed against her abdomen, it felt like an eternity passing.

Suddenly, there was the boy, riding the bird made of wind, landing gently in front of Aara. She knelt, cradling his face in her lap, and began chanting the spells she knew to counteract ill will. While she didn't know black magic or how to dispel it, she knew how to protect those she loved from its effects.

"Stop, Aara. Stop chanting the protection spell for the boy. How will you survive absorbing the poison of the vicious snake, made powerful enough to kill? I know you can't let the child die, but think of yourself as well. Think of Aameen, how will he live with himself, knowing you promised you would be alright? How will he bear it if you find your life so insignificant as to sacrifice it for just anyone?" Vaani's voice was pleading. "I heard him. I heard the old man. He was vicious and evil. This child might be part of his plan to destroy everything you have worked for, to shatter the faith, will, and compassion you have inspired in these people. This entire scheme was meant to end you. Why are you playing into his hands? You have to let the child go."

"You know I can't do that," Aara said with a sigh. "I cannot let the child die so that I can live. How could I go on, knowing I had the power to save him and chose myself over him? How would I face myself, Vaani?" With that, Aara closed her eyes, and absorbed the last of the pain and poison from the boy's body into her own, then collapsed.

In the village, the child opened his eyes as Aameen saw Aara fall to the ground, her face lifeless, turning pale, and blue. He pushed through the crowd, lifted Aara into his arms, and ran with all his strength. She had done it again; she had risked her life to save someone. He knew without question that it was the child. He knew Aara would go to any length to save a life, especially after the pain of losing their unborn child. She would never let another parent endure such anguish.

There was no anger or rage in Aameen's heart for Aara's sacrifice. He understood her boundless love and empathy for everyone she held dear. This village had given them the warmth and love of a family that they had never received from their own. Both he and Aara were willing to face whatever fate had in store to protect their people. Without uttering a word, though he could hear the villagers following behind him, calling out, and praying for Aara's safety, he prayed with all his being that the villagers' prayers and his would be answered—that Aara would survive.

He reached his cottage and kicked open the gate to the backyard. He placed Aara gently on the ground and went to lock the door. He didn't want the people to see what Aara was going through. If magic could save her, he intended to keep his promise of never letting another soul come near Aara when she was vulnerable. Her pulse weakened, and her breathing became deep and rapid, as if life was slipping away from her.

Aameen trembled with fear at the thought of losing Aara. "Don't you dare leave me alone, Aara. You are the love of my life, and my life would lose its meaning if you were to leave me behind in this world. You cannot die. You cannot die like this..." Aameen's sobs and tears seemed endless, just as Aara's pain, which she endured silently. She knew that if she let out a cry, Aameen would be unable to bear seeing her in such agony.

Aara called out, not to Vaani, but to the mother. Not her own mother, but the Mother of all: the elements of nature and the supreme being who nurtures the world. The one who had made her capable of receiving the blessings and power to protect and nurture those around her, spreading love, and compassion wherever she went. In that moment, as she called for help, Aara asked for the safety of Aameen, the people of the village, and the small boy she had just saved. With that, Aara exhaled one long, final breath, and then there was silence.

"You are beautiful, Aara," said a voice, a woman's voice, but not Vaani's. "I have blessed many and placed my trust in many, but you, my dear child, are my true child. My heart ached seeing you in pain, yet you embraced it with open arms, all to save that little boy. People pray to the four elements that create life, but you, Aara, have embodied them with your whole heart. You breathe them in and exhale them for the betterment of those around you. I bless you for the days to come, but even I cannot fight against death. All who are born must eventually perish to make way for new life.

"However, to shield you from the evil beings and demons who prey upon your motherly instincts, I grant you a power: whoever dares to kill you shall be cursed, transformed into a tree, forever rooted to the spot where he stands. He will remain bound for eternity until he finds a way to seek your forgiveness; only then will he be granted release and death. Immortality is a vice that humans should not pursue. Mortality is a blessing that people often overlook—it is mortality that brings humanity, compassion, and love. Knowing they will die one day teaches them to live fully today and be their best selves."

Aara felt a gentle kiss on her forehead as the voice of the Mother faded away.

Aara gained consciousness and saw Aameen crouched at the far end of the door. Aameen was trembling and crying. "Aameen," Aara called softly. "Will you keep thinking of the things you should have told me, or will you come here, hold me, and tell me every one of them, now that I am awake…" Aara looked at Aameen with a loving and mischievous smile. Aameen rushed to embrace her in a warm hug. He did scold her for a minute or two for making him so anxious and scared, but looking at Aara's face, all he could say was "I am so glad you're well and alive."

Aara didn't tell Aameen about the old man or the events in the shadowy forest where she had been transported, nor did she mention the Mother, the supreme being who blessed her with a protective shield to deter future evils in the difficult times to come. She wanted to spare him those fears, at least for the time being.

The warmth of Aameen's embrace wrapped her like a cocoon, and Aara could feel the steady beat of his heart and the unspoken love radiating from him. Despite the ache coursing through her body, Aara found comfort in that moment, enveloped in the simple purity of their shared love.

Aameen carried Aara to their room and gently laid her to rest on the bed. Stepping outside to reassure the worried crowd gathered at their doorstep, he felt an overwhelming tug of urgency to return to her, to hold her close. Once he had calmed the anxious gathering and sent them back to their homes, he bolted the door, urgency written on his face and in his eyes.

Aara looked at him with an inquisitive mind, and Aameen's smile gave him away. She knew exactly what was on his mind. It had been months since they had spent time together as a married couple. Aara shifted to her side of the bed, inviting Aameen with open arms.

The first caress on her cheek, and though the pain still throbbed through Aara's body, it no longer bothered her. All she wanted was Aameen and his touch. Aameen seemed to understand the needs of a weary soul, his soulmate, and gently cupped her face with both hands. He placed a kiss on her forehead, then on her eyes. Aameen cherished what he had: a beautiful, delicate, yet fiercely strong woman, the most remarkable he had ever known. And that woman was his. Her heart, soul, and body belonged to him, as his was hers.

With the warmth of Aameen's lips and breath, so close to her head, then her eyes, nose, and lips, Aara felt herself melting into the moment. Aameen had always approached her with a softness that spoke volumes. His eyes reflected tenderness, even as his body ached for something wilder. Helpless against his growing desire, Aameen tried to restrain himself, holding Aara's shoulders as his head rested against hers. His breathing grew heavier and deeper, a silent plea for her to accept him completely, without hesitation.

Aara held Aameen's hands, stopping them from sliding away. Gently, she tugged them back to her shoulders and smiled, a silent confirmation that she wanted him just as much. Aameen felt a surge of happiness, as though he had found the answer to his deepest prayers. He kissed Aara, letting go of everything that had held him back until then.

He loved her wholly, with all her elements, as she would often say. Aameen smiled to himself, marvelling at how incredible this woman was. Her generosity, kindness, and compassion in places where others might feel only hate or bitterness made her wonderful, inside, and out. Most of all, he cherished her unwavering devotion to him. It struck him how deeply she respected him, how dutifully she had always abided by what he asked of her, and yet she remained her own person, full of grace, and strength.

Remembering the day they had first met, Aameen couldn't deny the undeniable spark their souls had shared, even though both had initially refused to acknowledge it. Since that moment, they had both wholeheartedly, and selflessly invested in their relationship. Their mutual love and respect had grown stronger with each passing day, evolving them into a perfect fit for one another. Every challenge thrown their way had only granted them the opportunity to deepen their bond.

That night, they embarked on the purest and most surreal experience for both of them. Aameen's love, both fierce, and protective, redefined his own sense of self, while Aara found solace, and renewal in the depths of their union. Their relation evolved them into becoming their true selves, and the two souls now stood forever transformed, bound by selfless love, and devotion.

Chapter 5

Rose found solace in seeing Aara and Aameen together. The love they shared and the respect they held for one another were truly inspiring. Rose admired Aara's perseverance in saving the child, even though her own life was at jeopardy, and then the strength with which she weathered the storm without losing control or giving up. How gracefully she conquered her fears and came out alive.

"Anant, I understand what Aara has been trying to tell me about why she decided to create you. I know she wanted women like me to realize that one mustn't feel alone and helpless; it's all about believing in oneself and standing by one's sense of knowing. Like Aara, each of us must go through storms, for they shape us, as you said before. The hurdles and struggles are there to bring us closer to our true selves."

"To be honest," Rose continued, "the moment I saw the fire, the threat I felt wasn't about my safety but about the life I've built for myself. For years, my solitude stemmed from the fact that I had created something meaningful for myself, forgotten about the trials I faced, and focused instead on where I stood today. Aara reignited the feeling I had that night before running away from Tapas and the torments he put me through. I wanted to rebuild my life, driven by a self-belief sprouting from the hope of deserving better, a second chance at life to make it truly worth living."

Anant quietly listened to her and glowed with warmth. "Rose, moving forward, you need to tread your path carefully. In every moment, in every instance where you feel drawn, be wise. Try to learn to read the wind, the sound of nature whistling around you. There are no lies, only truth hidden beneath fear and insecurities. The only way to avoid becoming prey to vicious beings is to understand the cause and reason, strengthen your core, and move head-on into the battlefield. You are not alone. You have the whole world conspiring to bring you closer to yourself, your true potential, your magic."

"If you ask me," Anant said with a smile in his voice, "go out for your walks in the woods with Naazuk, like you used to. She will help you take a step closer to your next quest. Listen and understand the story ahead with a strong will to learn, evolve, and adapt. The answers to the riddles going around in your head lie somewhere close by, but they will require a willing heart to untangle and absorb the magic concealed within the lines."

Rose nodded like an obedient child listening to their favourite teacher and opened the book again. As she turned the next page, her expression changed drastically. She saw Aameen running through the woods, his clothes soaked in blood and his face bruised. His arms and legs were wounded, as was his left eye, with blood everywhere. His steps were uncertain and frantic, like those of a child lost in the dark woods.

"Where are you, Aara?" he screamed, crying. "Where did they take you?" Aameen yelled in anger and hurt, falling to the ground, his hands covering his face.

Something had gone terribly wrong, she thought to herself. Rose hurriedly turned the page.

But the page was blank. Rose couldn't hold herself back. She brushed her hand over the blank page and closed her eyes. "Anant, take me to Aara. I want to see where she is. I know we are connected somehow, so I summon her, just like she always did. I want to see her. I want to make sure she's safe." Rose murmured the summoning spell she had learned from Aara.

The wind rushed in from the window beside Rose, and she saw dried leaves starting to swirl around her.

In the blink of an eye, Rose found Aara in front of her. She was in a dark, dingy place, far from soil, trees, or water, only air, but even that was stuffy from lack of ventilation. Rose coughed to ease her throat. To her surprise, Aara raised her head, and looked at her.

"Vaani, is that you?" Aara asked inquisitively.

"No, no... no, no. I'm Rose. I was reading your story... I mean, Anant was narrating your story to me. How did I get here?!" Rose looked around frantically. She remembered summoning Aara, but perhaps because Aara was much more powerful than her, she had somehow transported herself into another lifetime and ended up with Aara instead. "Oh, my head is dizzy. Where am I?" Rose looked around, full of confusion.

Aara stared at Rose. "I don't know why you're calling yourself Rose when I've been hearing your voice all my life, and I know it belongs to Vaani," Aara said with a sceptical look on her face.

Rose, taken aback, remembered what Anant had told her. She needed to regain her composure. She, too, was magic, as Anant had always said, and now she believed it. She remembered seeing Aameen wounded. There was no time to waste. She had to bring Aara to safety.

"We'll talk later, Aara. I have just as many questions as you do, but this is not the time to lose focus," Rose said with newfound confidence. She needed to get Aara out of this place.

"The will to protect shall always be greater and stronger than the power to destroy," Rose reiterated the words with a smile on her face. She closed her eyes and raised her arms, her hands forming a mudra she had learned from Aara to invoke Mother Nature, seeking enlightenment, and help.

Aara, as surprised as she was, understood there was no time to question but to act. She joined Rose, and together they chanted spells to awaken the land beneath. They called upon the trees surrounding the earth. They knew that trees and grass couldn't be far.

The two women, united in their sole purpose to break free from captivity, evoked the roots of the ancient forest. As their powers merged, Rose and Aara felt something shifting beneath the surface. Aara pulled Rose into a corner, and Rose unknowingly held Aara in her arms in a protective gesture.

Within minutes, everything became quiet again. They both, holding hands, stepped forward to see what had happened. To their surprise, roots had erupted everywhere, causing cracks in the cave's floor and walls. A stream of moonlight filtered through, inviting them to follow. Aara and Rose exchanged a pleased look. They had found their way out.

Once outside in the open, they both breathed deeply. Aara immediately recognized the smell of the soil. It was the same forest where the old evil priest had trapped her. The metallic taste in her mouth and the pungent smell of black magic were unmistakable. Aara feared for Rose's safety.

Aara recognized the magic in Rose. She was like her mirror image, though still sprouting, not yet in full bloom. Aara thought to herself how this person was identical to Vaani yet different in ways she couldn't pinpoint. Brushing the thought aside for later, Aara requested Rose to return to wherever she had come from. It was not safe for a human to be there, especially someone who didn't belong in this world.

Rose couldn't help but stare at Aara with wonder in her eyes. "You are so beautiful, Aara. So precious. I don't know why or how I ended up here, but now that I am, I can't leave you like this. I will not be at peace with myself," Rose said apologetically.

Aara, with confusion in her eyes, didn't ask Rose anything but began narrating the events that had led to her captivity. "There were fires in the forest close to my village. Three of the assailants were spotted near the village well, and the villagers ran to capture them. Little did they know it was a distraction. Four more of them began setting fire to the villagers' cottages, and then chaos erupted. People ran frantically. It was a planned chaos to create fear and distract them from noticing that I was being kidnapped," Aara said with a sigh of disappointment. "I was in my cottage when I heard the screams. The next thing I noticed was a strong metallic smell..." Aara paused and looked at Rose. "...like this land reeks of. It's the smell of black magic."

Aara explained to Rose how the smell of nature vanishes in places where evil thoughts and ill will prevail. "Where powers are evoked not to protect or nurture but to cause destruction and chaos to establish supremacy. This is the land of the evil priest, and we must leave as soon as possible."

Rose understood well what Aara was referring to. Aara, seeing the knowing look on Rose's face, continued, "I did my best in the cave, but my powers seemed dampened. I couldn't summon any of the elements to aid me until you arrived and reignited the fire within me to try again, harder this time. I have always respected Vaani, but seeing you here in physical form... I am overwhelmed with gratitude."

"I am not Vaani. My name is Rose. You don't know me, but I know everything about you," Rose tried to explain compassionately. "I don't know how I got here, but I remember chanting the spell you use to summon someone in need. Instead of bringing you to safety, as I thought the spell would do, I got transported to your world."

Rose described seeing Aameen hurt and frantically searching for Aara. She could see Aara's rage building.

"You must return to wherever you've come from. Just know that you are my Vaani. You may be Rose in your world, but in my world, you are my guiding star." Saying this, Aara began chanting a protective spell for Rose, calling her Vaani. "You must stay safe and remember: we can only truly be there for others when we have faith in ourselves and are fully present for ourselves."

Rose felt herself falling back into her chair at the Rays, her eyes wide open.

Anant took a deep breath and said he was glad she made it back in time. Before her eyes, Rose saw the pages coming to life: a dark forest surrounding Aara where Rose had left her. Aara looked straight towards her and said in a loud voice, "Tell me, Vaani, where to find Aameen." Rose was surprised by the tugging urge inside her to speak. Shaken and confused, she nevertheless decided to ask aloud, "Can you hear me, Aara?"

"Yes, Vaani, I can hear you loud and clear. Now, please guide me. Close your eyes and tell me exactly what you saw," Aara said, looking at Rose as if she could see her. Rose focused and reiterated all the minute details she remembered about Aameen before he collapsed on the ground. As she turned the page, she saw the yellow pages turning light green, and Aara was magically transported to the spot Rose had described. Aara wasn't surprised by the magic; however, Rose was spellbound. Somehow, the realization dawned on her that she was more connected and entwined with the story than she had comprehended.

Rose turned the page as Anant, after remaining quiet for so long, resumed the narration. Rose made a face. "Let's pretend I have become delusional, right, Anant?"

"You are more than everything you ever imagined, Rose. Keep faith in yourself and understand who you are and the depth of your powers," Anant replied.

As Aara went on to search for Aameen, Rose could see he had been captured by assailants and was bound to the old white ash tree just outside the dark forest. "Aara, run to the east side of where you stand. An old white ash tree holds Aameen trapped on its trunk," Rose said urgently.

The priest was there; Rose could see him standing in the shadows. Something was off about the whole thing, like a laid-up trap. Rose focused harder, remembering the mysterious power the wind held. If the wind could magically transport her to Aara, it could also rustle the shrubs and bushes around Aameen to reveal what was really happening there.

"I believe in myself, and I believe in the magic within me. May the wind be my guard and companion, and show me the true colours of the shadow before my eyes," Rose murmured with her eyes closed and then blew air on the right page where she could see Aameen tied to the tree. A rush of wind came whooshing in, bending the branches of the trees and rustling the shrubs around. Rose saw men hiding in plain sight around Aameen. The priest knew Aara would break free from the cave. This was a setup to make Aara sacrifice herself. Rose understood the entire plan.

The evil priest knew that whoever killed Aara would be cursed. They would be mortified into becoming a tree, bound to the land, living through eternity in repentance. The curse would force them to endure the seasons, shedding everything they knew, and facing the torment of their deeds. The cycle would never end until forgiven by Aara herself. In pursuit of a way out, the priest decided to capture Aameen and torture Aara into ending her own life.

Little did he know, Aara couldn't kill herself. She stood her ground, protecting others, and was blessed with the strength to withstand any pain or trauma.

What Aara and Rose didn't realize was that the great white ash tree was bound by magic. The place reeked of black magic, holding Aara in the centre with no power to evoke her magic. Exhausted from trying to unbind Aameen, Aara fell to her knees.

"What have I ever done to you that you make me feel so helpless? Who are you, and why do you carry so much hatred for me inside you?" Aara asked, weeping.

"It is not who you are but what you are capable of," said the evil priest, emerging from the shadows. Laughing to himself, he continued, "You are a woman. The audacity, I am appalled. How dare you challenge my power, my supremacy? People begged at my door for mercy, and you ruined it all. These villagers stopped coming because of you. They stopped praying to me. They were getting everything for free!" The rage in the priest's eyes flared.

The priest confessed to orchestrating the chaos and laughed until only the echo of his voice remained. Aara, helpless, said, "I know you wish for me to end my life. But that is not possible. I cannot let my choices harm Aameen further."

Seeing Aara's torment, Aameen gathered his strength, and decided to end the misfortune. "I will kill Aara with my own hands," Aameen said bitterly, tears streaming down his face.

"No, Aameen! What are you saying? Did you not understand the curse my murderer will bear?" Aara pleaded.

Aameen, with a heavy heart, replied, "I cannot see you die bit by bit, Aara. My dignity lies in saving you, even at the cost of my life."

The evil priest, fascinated by Aameen's resolve, released him from the ash tree. A sword was handed to Aameen, and Aara was brought before him. Aameen kissed her one last time and, apologizing, drove the sword into her gut.

And then there was only silence.

Rose turned the next page, but it was blank. Her face wet with tears, she was horrified by what had unfolded. Hugging the book close to her chest, Rose cried, mourning the deaths of Aara and Aameen. Anant remained silent, cold, as he too relived the horrifying events.

Chapter 6

Rose couldn't sleep that night, twisting, and turning in her bed. She couldn't ease the pain in her heart after seeing Aara silently accept her fate. Aara had promised herself to live by Aameen's side and respect his decisions, and Aameen, too, couldn't be blamed for his choice. Nobody, even in their worst nightmare, would wish to see their loved ones endure such a horrifying death. Rose pulled Anant out from under her cushion and hugged him tightly.

"Anant… why?" Rose sobbed.

The book warmed up in her embrace, and Anant said hearteningly, "Rose, sometimes bad things happen, and there is no rhyme or reason for it. But Aara and Aameen, even at the end, stood by what they truly believed in, and that's all that matters."

"But the story doesn't end there, and that's where I come into the picture. Aara began creating me when she first understood the nature of life and death as two sides of the same coin. Under the guidance of Vaani, Aara breathed life into me. I became witness to the magic they created within themselves and the magic they spread willingly with open arms thereafter."

Rose remembered Anant asking her to go for walks in the woods with Naazuk.

"Anant, are these woods, the forest behind Ray's residence, somehow related?" Rose asked innocently.

Then it struck her.

"Is Aameen still here in this world, trapped? The curse!

The curse must have turned Aameen into a tree, trapped for generations…" Rose's eyes widened with the realization.

Anant sighed. "Yes, Rose… now listen carefully." He began narrating what happened next:

After taking the life of the one he loved the most, time stood still for Aameen. He couldn't move as Aara's lifeless body lay limp in his trembling hands, stained with her blood. The sword he had wielded to end her suffering fell from his grip, clattering against the earth as he bent to place her gently on the ground.

She was part of Mother Nature, he told himself. Sobbing, he begged the Mother, the one Aara always prayed to, to protect her, for he could do nothing more. He prayed for Aara to be engulfed in peace so that no mortal could ever harm her again. He pleaded for her never to be born again, to avoid the endless cycle of life and death where she would have to prove her worth over and over. He asked that she remain above it all, at peace forever.

Weeping bitterly, Aameen prayed for his own death, unable to bear a life without Aara by his side. He couldn't imagine waking to a day when she wouldn't smile at him with her loving eyes.

Suddenly, a peculiar warmth began to emanate from the ground beneath them. A brilliant green light pulsed around Aara's body, and the earth seemed to breathe. Roots emerged, weaving themselves gently around her, cradling her form as though the land itself wanted to hold her one last time.

Aameen then heard a deep, resonant voice echoing, asking him to weep no more. It came from the ancient ash tree where he had been held captive minutes ago.

The tree confessed that it was moved by Aameen's love and his decision to take upon himself the curse of being bound by the earth forever, all to ensure that Aara could die with dignity and not at the hands of evil. The earth, in turn, vowed to hold his soul dear. The ash tree bowed in devotion to his love and sacrifice, promising to shelter Aameen, and preserve him until he attained salvation from the curse.

The voice continued, acknowledging Aara's selflessness, and the good she had done for others. Every act, no matter how small, had been for the betterment of the people. Even at the end, she upheld her promises, silently accepting her fate. The Mother accepted Aameen's prayer. Aara would live on, not as a being, human, animal, or bird, but as a part of the elements she was so deeply connected to. Anyone born thereafter with magic in their heart could pray to her and speak to her. However, she would never be reborn, for she had fulfilled her life's purpose.

Relief washed over Aameen. With teary eyes, he kissed Aara one last time. The roots intertwined with her body, and her fresh wounds began to close. The forest came alive with the scent of wildflowers and the freshness of the rain. The oppressive stench of black magic lifted as the light grew brighter. The land embraced her, absorbing her into its essence.

Closing his eyes, Aameen felt the branches of the ash tree pulling him towards its mighty trunk. They engulfed him, as if accepting his fate. He did not open his eyes again."

"Years passed, and generations came, and went. Aameen lies here still, waiting in exile to be liberated and reunited with Aara," Anant shared.

He then elaborated on Naazuk and her visions.

"Naazuk is an incarnation of Aara's eldest sister, the first to be blessed by Aara and her magic. Naazuk doesn't understand why her visions are always of forests or why she feels compelled to paint them; it's her way of igniting life within them. Through those visions and paintings, Rose, you can find the great ash tree and Aameen. And only you can unshackle him from this curse."

"So, I truly am Vaani?" Rose asked. "Aara was right?"

Anant responded with glowing warmth, "Yes, my dear. You are the echo that guided Aara in another life, and in this one, Aara became the echo of belief for you to find yourself. You two, bound by the same star, were always meant to guide one another. Sisters not by blood, but by fate. As Aara has helped you find your inner strength, it is now your turn to help the love of her life find salvation and forever be hers."

Rose stayed quiet for a long time until she drifted off to sleep. The fears that had kept her awake the previous night were no longer there. She could see many things more clearly now. She somehow understood that even the presence of Tapas and his interference in her life, shackling her reality, were things meant to be, challenges she was destined to face.

This was where she was supposed to be. She was meant to find refuge with Naazuk Ray, and with her strength, and inner power, she would fight this evil and not let it prevail, even in this lifetime.

She had to make sure she stood her ground, just as Aara, and Aameen had. She needed to remember who she was and move forward on her journey with unwavering faith and belief. No longer could she hide or suppress who she was and what she was capable of.

And yes, she had to find Aameen. She would find him, and somehow, the belief warmed her heart. She knew when the time came, she would discover a way to free him.

Chapter 7

When Rose woke up the next day, the memories of her past seemed to have faded away. She felt anew. She felt lighter and motivated. She dressed up for office, but before that, she stood before the mirror, gazing at her reflection. She looked like Aara. Her eyes were no longer those of the girl who used to be broken or always led down. Her eyes held the confidence of the woman who had the strength to start anew, who had the will, and the power to face the evil in his eyes and claim what was hers. Her life was in her hands, and she was no longer chained to her past.

Rose joined Ramanuj and Naazuk at the dining table, where they were sitting, and chatting, tea cups in hand. What a beautiful couple they are, Rose thought to herself, silently blessing them to always find solace in one another. From the worry in Naazuk's eyes, Rose guessed that Ramanuj must have shared details about Tapas with her. Being his wife, it was only natural that he had done so, and Rose wasn't upset. She would have done the same if the roles were reversed.

Naazuk, noticing Rose, changed her expression to appear cheerful. She didn't want to burden Rose with her worries or make her feel upset about her past. The couple had decided to be there for her, no matter what.

"Oh, here you are," Naazuk said with a warm smile, welcoming Rose. "Come have breakfast, dear," she added, pulling out a chair for her. "I was just about to make some pancakes. Please keep Ramanuj company and bear with his endless rants about politics.

I'm too bored with hearing the same complaints over and over," she teased with a laugh and headed to the kitchen.

"Rose, I've been in constant touch with the police," Ramanuj said with fatherly assurance in his eyes. "They'll find him in no time. This town is too small for a stranger to hide. Someone will surely tip off the authorities, and he'll be behind bars soon."

"I've also sent you some articles to review. You can go through them in our study," Ramanuj added, opening his laptop. After a brief pause, he apologetically added, "Naazuk and I think it would be best if you worked from home for a couple of days."

Rose smiled at Ramanuj; she well understood their kind intention. It was a conscious effort on their part to help her maintain a sense of normalcy. She said nothing, only nodded in agreement, appreciating their thoughtfulness.

Breakfast felt like a meal with family. Rose found herself smiling and laughing as Ramanuj and Naazuk shared their wonderful memories, filling her in on the years she had seemingly missed.

When Ramanuj left for work, Naazuk returned to the study where Rose was sitting with a laptop on her lap, her gaze vacantly looking outside. Naazuk gently asked if she wanted to step outside for a walk before sitting for work.

Rose looked at Naazuk with newfound warmth in her heart. She now understood why she always felt drawn to her and always wished for her happiness. Smiling wishfully, she asked, "Can I see your paintings before we step outside? I've always wanted to ask you about them. Can you show me around?".

"Oh, of course, I'd love to." Naazuk couldn't help but beam at the request. "It's rare to find someone who wants to spend time appreciating art. I am not much of an artist, but painting always brought me peace. I must confess, though, you'll only find trees, and forests in my work. I have always felt compelled to paint landscapes and dark woods. My dreams always find solace when they make their way onto my canvas, sketched, and brought to life with colours." Naazuk said nervously, rubbing her neck.

"You are a gifted artist, Naazuk," Rose replied sincerely. "Your paintbrushes are witnesses to the magic you create. And as far as painting nature is concerned, maybe that's exactly what you were meant to do. Maybe it's a blessing in disguise. Maybe... just maybe... You were always meant to guide those who have lost their way, help them find their path again."

Rose couldn't help but hug Naazuk in a warm, comforting embrace after saying this.

Tears welled up in Naazuk's eyes as she moved to hold Rose's hands in hers. Smiling softly, she thought to herself, here she was, trying to comfort Rose, yet it was Rose who filled her heart with the magic of self-belief.

Going from one wall to another, Rose was amazed by the intricacies and exquisite details that Naazuk had captured with her paintbrushes. They truly seemed dreamlike. Naazuk had mastered the art of bringing them to life. Absorbing and appreciating each minute stroke, Rose would look at the paintings and then at Naazuk, wondering how, and why she had never exhibited her work.

Feeling overwhelmed by Rose's response and the expression of amazement on her face, Naazuk quietly left Rose to continue exploring the paintings. She went to pack their lunch for a picnic outside, as it was almost noon. Naazuk felt an urge to take Rose to her favourite spot at the edge of the woods, assuming it might bring Rose the same sense of peace it always brought her.

Rose was happy appreciating Naazuk's work, but felt a little upset, sensing she had not yet seen any trace of the ancient tree described by Anant. As she turned back towards the study to check if she had received the assignment Ramanuj had mentioned, her gaze fell upon a large painting, framed in double glass, that seemed to be integrated into the door itself, leading to their main living room.

There it was: the ancient ash tree with its dark brown, enormous trunk, and branches so vast that thousands of lost souls could find shelter beneath them. Its size, even in the painting, made Rose's eyes widen with amazement. She had seen him. Rose smiled to herself contentedly.

"Naazuk, can you take me here?" Rose asked loudly, urgency in her voice.

Naazuk came out of the kitchen to see what Rose was talking about. Noticing her gaze fixed on the painting framed on the door to their living room, Naazuk spoke regretfully, "Ah, this one… I've never seen it with my own eyes—only in dreams, almost every night. I wish I had. It appeared in my most beautiful dreams but also in my worst nightmares. It haunted me for so many years that I had to paint it, and only then did it stop tormenting me in my sleep."

"You'll find many such trees in the forest nearby. Don't look so disheartened," Naazuk chirped.

Rose asked herself to be patient.

On the other side of town, someone noticed a tall man with a hunchback, desperately smoking cigarette after cigarette and checking his watch repeatedly. Recognizing his face from the posters near the police station, the observer quickly called the police to report the suspicious-looking stranger. While on the call, the person hurriedly informed the police that two men had just joined the stranger. The observer immediately recognized them as local goons, infamous in town for causing trouble purely for amusement.

The police instructed the caller to stay away but to keep an eye on the group and notify them if they left his sight. However, by the time the police arrived, the men had already gone. Realizing that the suspect had already made allies, likely paying them handsomely given that their meeting had taken place in one of the town's poshest cafés, the officer alerted his team to remain extra vigilant.

Chapter 8

After returning from her walk with Naazuk, Rose felt calmer. She enjoyed Naazuk's company and her childlike nature. Naazuk was a blessed soul who could find happiness even in the tiniest of things and seemed amazed as she strolled through unpaved trails, finding new spots to store in her memory for her next paintings.

Back in her room, Rose took Anant in her hands and decided to learn more about him, wondering if something from the past could help her navigate this phase and find answers to the quest before her.

"Tell me about yourself, Anant. How did you come into being? Also, how come for so many years, nobody could read, or decipher the wonders of magic you had hidden in plain sight? I wonder what would have happened if these spells were practised by someone with ill intent". Rose paused, "Do you also know anything about who I am… I trust Aara's judgment, but how can I be Vaani? I know nothing about life." Rose suddenly felt sullen, for she could see her bad decisions and memories flashing before her eyes, as compared to Aara, who always had complete faith in herself.

Anant warmed in her hands and replied to Rose in a calm voice, "Aara and Vaani were magical beings who decided to put their knowledge into words. Though they could perform spells to protect, nurture, and inspire people to find their true selves and support one another, every coin has a flip side. The same elements of nature, land, water, fire, and air that constitute life can be manipulated to take it away if used with devious intent. So, I had to be protected.

"Right after the snake incident, Vaani realized that the devious priest had somehow gained knowledge of the scripture Aara was creating. First, his reputation was at stake, and second, his greed for power and supremacy made him more malicious. The snake incident, devised to trap, and kill Aara, was the tipping point. After much contemplation, Vaani offered a solution. She instructed Aara to encrypt me. Through magic, the words were mingled, and only stories of how to nurture one another through simple water prayers and meditation were left, enough for me to avoid being deemed useless and discarded.

"Thinking back, perhaps that's how it has always been with you and others. Your blessings upon people in need not only aided them in coming through their most difficult phase victorious, but also instilled in them a core personality of being compassionate towards others in need. As reciprocation, a blessing in disguise, some of those individuals then also became entitled to play roles in aiding you across lifetimes."

Anant smiled to himself and continued, "You remember, the young boy Aara saved from the venom of a vicious snake, feeling terrible knowing he was bitten on his tongue, Aara blessed him to become a master of languages, a polyglot, in future.

"Ever since that night, the boy felt a deep connection to her and vowed to dedicate his life in helping others in need, just as she always did. What Aara didn't know was that every night, the boy would also wish for an opportunity to repay the debt of saving his life.

"On the dreadful day when fires ravaged the village, that same boy came to Aara's rescue. Sensing the looming danger to her life, Aara bestowed upon the boy a protective shield to keep him safe from any harm, especially from the men brainwashed by the priest's malicious influence. She entrusted him with her life's work, instructing him to keep the scripture close to his heart, hidden from the world and to translate whatever he could, when he turns 62 years old.

"The boy grew into a highly learned and respected man in society. By then, he had developed exceptional linguistic skills and was a known professional in the field, but he never forgot Aara or the blessings she had given him; it remained deeply ingrained in his heart. On his 70th birthday, he finally opened the scripture, her sacred creation, and translated as much as he could into English. After his death, the book he had left nameless was published anonymously, though only a few copies were ever made.

"I remained dormant for centuries, waiting for fate to send the one I was meant for, the one destined to awaken me. Imagine my faith in Aara that I never questioned how long I was to wait or who I was meant for. I trusted fate and the divine."

Anant glowed with warmth, filling Rose's heart with a sense of belonging and letting her know that this was where he was meant to be, and she was the one he was meant to be with.

"What a relief it was when I first saw you. My purpose in life was right before my eyes. It was bittersweet to know that, like all lives once born, I, too, would perish. But knowing that I would fulfil the purpose of my awakening, that I would finally be home and at peace, made the journey absolutely worth it.

As for the mystery of who you are and how you came into Aara's life at such a young age, when she first heard your voice in her head… Rose, you have always been the embodiment of faith and belief that resides within humans. You are the gut feeling that compels one to choose what's right. When Aara lost her life untimely, balance had to be restored. The Mother, the Supreme, decided to send you to earth, making you human so you could help Aameen find redemption, and me, peace, at last."

Anant, understanding that they were so close to attaining their goal, decided not to withhold the last piece of information, which Rose somehow sensed was connected but couldn't quite place her finger on why or how.

"Like I have always tried to make you understand, Rose, every coin has a flip side. You, being the embodiment of goodness, intuition, willpower, and inner strength, extended your hand toward Aara to guide her in fulfilling her life's purpose. You knew and understood that she was your mirror image in the living world and that through her, you could do much greater good for people—instilling them with faith to trust their instincts, showing compassion to the needy, and providing the strength to fight against evil.

The ruler of sins, Asmodium, felt compelled to find someone so wronged by life that his heart would harbour nothing but hate, a hate so intense that he would feel no guilt in taking another's life. Asmodium used this person to spread his share of hatred in the living world. He found his prey in Bhariman, who was only 11 years old. This boy had been orphaned by the mass killing of innocents ordered by a ruler seeking to prove his superiority and power. To showcase his strength, the ruler commanded his soldiers to destroy village after village, including men, women, and children. None was spared, except for Bhariman, who had hidden under a cottage floor. His mother had sent him there to fetch coals for cooking.

Hearing the cries and feeling the splatter of blood on his face through the floorboards, Bhariman witnessed the massacre, the screams of his people, and the death of his family. He couldn't move but stayed hidden. Hidden through the killings and for years afterwards, as those who looked at him only showed pity, not compassion, to take him in. Around the same time Bhariman began hearing Asmodium's voice, you, Rose, started communicating with Aara.

While you trained Aara to strengthen her belief in herself and ignite the powers within her to protect and nurture humankind, Bhariman was being trained and empowered by Asmodium to use the same power to break people's wills and instil sin in their hearts. Lust, greed, wrath, envy, and pride spread wherever he went. Over the years, he began practising magic, but only to further his devious intentions.

When one of Bhariman's men heard about a boy named Aameen marrying a girl rumoured to possess supernatural powers, he immediately informed Asmodium. This set the plan in motion to eliminate the source of strength itself. Asmodium already knew about Vaani. He knew you were guiding a mortal, but the face of this mortal had remained unknown until then. Now, he had learned her identity and resolved to end her.

The man who informed Bhariman was one of the two friends who had come to see Aara for marriage to Aameen under Bhariman's instructions. This same man, despite being part of Aameen's crew, succumbed to the greed instilled by Bhariman and informed them about the stall and Aara's pregnancy. He was the one who aided the assailants in killing Aameen's troop and later came to kill Aara at the cottage when Aameen was away. Aara somehow escaped their clutches but couldn't fight for long.

After Aara's death, Bhariman continued his reign of wrath and evil for months, but like all living beings, his life was marked with numbered heartbeats, and he too met his end. In his final days, Asmodium abandoned him. Bhariman couldn't understand why and assumed it was because there was nothing left for him to learn. He believed he had surpassed Asmodium himself. Pride, the final sin, had taken root, and ultimately brought him closer to his demise.

Hearing of the atrocities in the forests controlled by this evil priest, nearby kingdoms joined forces to end his reign of terror.

Captured, tied, and left to rot in a dungeon, Bhariman decided to summon Asmodium one last time to make a final wish. Asmodium, unable to deny his most loyal servant, listened. Fuelled by hatred for seeing people happy, having families, and caring for one another, something no one had done for him, Bhariman made his wish. In pure spite, he asked Asmodium to bring him back to life when a magical being re-entered the realm of the living. Asmodium quietly granted his dying wish. That is Tapas Amin."

Chapter 9

Rose stayed in bed until late evening that day. The weight of Anant's confessions from hours ago still pressed heavily on her thoughts, and she had no intention of seeing anyone until she could at least set a few things straight for herself.

She woke to the sound of a knock on her door. I must have drifted off while thinking, she thought. The knock grew louder, harder than usual.

Without giving it much thought, Rose decided to trust her instincts. Whoever was on the other side of the door was certainly not one of the Rays. She closed her eyes and chanted the protective spell, casting a shield over herself that made her invisible. She then moved to sit silently in the corner of the bed. *No movement, no sound,* she told herself.

A couple of minutes passed before someone snorted from downstairs and shouted in a loud voice, "Just break the goddamn door... What are you waiting for?! I can't just sit here watching them bleed to death. We've created enough ruckus for the sum paid. Just get the girl so we can call an ambulance for these two and leave." He ended with a laugh.

Rose froze.

The door was banged open, and a tall, dark man in his early 20s stormed into the room. Though not particularly muscular, he appeared like an average young man with a lean body and ruffled hair, almost as if he had lost his way and mistakenly ended up at the Rays' residence. Absent-mindedly, he tossed things around, his movements disjointed, and uninterested. Even his effort to check the washroom seemed forced.

Fortunately, his boredom made him disinclined to inspect the other side of the bed, which, under plain sight, appeared empty. Had he taken a closer look, he might have noticed a faint haze, just enough to arouse suspicion.

"She's not here," the man in the room shouted for his partner to hear.

But then, how was the door bolted from inside? he wondered, but he quickly brushed it aside, assuming the door must have gotten stuck somehow.

The two men seemed to make themselves at home, assuming Rose must have stepped out and would return soon enough. Laughing, they remarked how she had nowhere else to go. Considering she hadn't been seen since the boss burned her place down, the men were content to wait patiently. The muffled sounds coming from directly below made Rose guess they were sitting at the dining table, in the room adjacent to the lobby, making any escape through the front door next to impossible.

Rose knew she didn't have much time. She overheard one of them saying it was a good decision to wait here instead. They had left the couple in the drawing room, apparently not wanting to watch them panting and drifting into unconsciousness, likely to die from blood loss. The thought sent a shudder through Rose.

Tiptoeing to the end of the stairs, Rose strained to hear them talk, hoping for a moment when they might look away so she could run outside for help. She cursed herself for being so ignorant and not staying on her toes. When she and Naazuk had returned from their walk, Rose thought she would quickly freshen up before coming down for tea, which Naazuk had offered as soon as they arrived. She had put her phone on charge and gone to her room, only to be drawn into a conversation with Anant that took her into another dimension. She hadn't realized how much time had passed. All said and done, the couple was tied, much to Rose's relief, though their condition was dire. Naazuk had suffered a head injury, likely from being pushed into a table. At the same time, Ramanuj was severely bruised, having been battered with kicks and punches for any information about Rose's whereabouts. Tears rolled down Rose's cheeks as rage and fury surged within her. Neither of them could see her; she was still cloaked in the protective shield.

Standing at the threshold, Rose faced a decision. She could remain invisible, walk to the couple, and make her presence felt, perhaps giving them strength to hold on a little longer while waiting for the men to leave on their own. But there was no guarantee they would survive, given the time, and blood already lost. Alternatively, she could unveil herself, and face the men, hoping they might show the kindness they occasionally hinted at, saving the Rays in time but leaving Rose to face her fate. The thought of dying with the guilt of failing her purpose, helping Aara and Aameen find redemption and love, was unbearable.

Then Rose did something she hadn't considered a moment ago. She closed her eyes and prayed to the elements—air, land, fire, and water—both within and around her. Letting her mind wander beyond the door, she focused on the outside sounds: the roads, the chatter, the buzz of the streets. Filtering out the noise, she prayed to find what she sought. Suddenly, she heard it—a siren, though not from a patrol car but a fire engine. She latched onto the sound, relying on it to create a spark of fear in the men downstairs. Rose focused her will, amplifying the siren's volume in her mind and channelling it outward with the wind. The sound grew louder and clearer, as if it were just outside.

She was right. Despite their relaxed demeanour, the siren caused the men to flinch. Eyes wide, they sprang from their chairs.

"Bloody hell! What's that? Do you think someone heard the clattering and thrashing?" the tall man asked, fear evident in his voice.

"I don't know… oh hell. We should leave. It's reason enough to go without the girl, don't you think?" the shorter, stockier man replied.

They exchanged a look, and within a minute, they grabbed their jackets from the drawing room. Glancing one last time at the couple, one of them said, "I'm sorry, Mr. Ray, that it's come to this. You've been good to us… but you understand, don't you? Money is life. Tell the girl we'll be back for her. If not today, then tomorrow. If not us, someone else will. She might've had a fighting chance with us; we could've helped her, like you always helped us…"

The tall man cut him off with a sharp glance. "Throw her out. She deserves what's coming. That lunatic won't let her be and won't mind spreading brutality on everyone around her just to drag her to him."

With that, they searched for their cigarettes, rushed outside, and disappeared into the empty street, the imagined siren still loud in their heads, compelling them to flee.

As soon as the men were out on the street and no longer in her vision, Rose broke the chanting and spell, and hurried to the couple. Without thinking much, she called the emergency service in haste and cut the call.

"What hell have I brought upon you two?" Rose couldn't help but start weeping with desperation. Seeing the two people who meant more to her than her own family ever had, in such a dire situation, only in pursuance to protect her, it broke loose an end she never knew she had in her. She placed a hand on Naazuk's shoulder and asked where the medicines were. Everything else could wait.

By the time the ambulance arrived, followed by a police wagon, Rose was reassured by the officer-in-charge, Mr. Begh, that she had done the right thing. Had she surrendered herself to those men, there was no way of knowing if the couple would have survived, such men could never be trusted to spare a life, let alone save one. Rose nodded silently.

The couple was strapped to stretchers and taken to the hospital for proper bandaging and care. The nurse tending to them told Rose that the injuries on Ramanuj seemed brutal but didn't appear to have been inflicted with the intent to kill. Rose understood that the purpose was likely to extract information, but it still shouldn't have happened in the first place.

She knew she needed to think on her feet and get this mess sorted immediately. After answering the police's questions and providing a brief description of the two men, they advised Rose to find a safe place to stay and not spend the night at the Ray residence, as there was a high chance the men would return. Rose nodded in compliance and closed the door behind her.

It was only after she received a call from the hospital informing her that both Naazuk and Ramanuj were stable but under sedatives and would remain in the hospital overnight that Rose finally closed her eyes and let out a long sigh. She told herself, it's time. No more hiding. This is my battle, and I will fight it alone.

It was around midnight when Rose called Mr. Begh on his personal phone. Apologizing for calling him at such a late hour, she shared that she was still at the Rays' residence and, despite much thought, had failed to find anywhere else to go. The idea of involving others and putting their lives in jeopardy haunted her.

Mr. Begh could hear weariness in Rose's voice. Understanding the vulnerability of the situation, he silently agreed, and urged her to remain vigilant. There was no point in introducing herself to strangers around the town and checking into a hotel. He knew too well that people could be bought for mere pennies.

He informed her that, anticipating such a situation, he had already stationed two officers nearby to monitor the area and intervene in case of any break-in attempts. Before ending the call, Mr. Begh felt obliged to share some information about the two men. He told her the two attackers were known to be petty criminals — standard goons whose track record included theft and intimidating people for money on behalf of loan sharks. However, this level of violence and manhandling was completely out of character for them.

Mr. Begh admitted his disbelief, remarking that it was difficult to accept that these men would target Ramanuj Ray, the very person who had been financially supporting their families since they ran away from their homes. "Anyone else, perhaps, but for them to raise their hands against Ramanuj? It's baffling," he said, his voice tinged with disbelief.

After ending the call, Rose reflected on his words. She recalled hearing the short, plump man suggest calling for emergency help for the Rays as the taller man stepped out of her room. Deep down, she sensed that these men might have been manipulated, pawns in Tapas's scheme to scare and corner her.

Rose had more than one reason to conclude that she should stay for one more night. She resolved that when Naazuk returned the next day, she would apologize for the catastrophe that had engulfed them due to her presence and leave immediately. Though she had nowhere to go and her home was still weeks away from being ready, she decided she would find a hotel on the outskirts and stay there for the time being. The other reason compelled her to act immediately, leaving no time for doubt or hesitation.

Her thoughts were interrupted by the sudden ring of the landline, startling her. Her gut churned with dread, but she quickly made her way downstairs to answer the call.

"Look, I found you! Did you enjoy my surprise?" Tapas's voice came through the receiver, laced with a sinister chuckle, as if he were playing a prank. His tone was calm and composed, almost like that of an old friend. "Aren't you going to greet me or tell me you missed me too… and maybe, apologize for causing so much pain to me?" he continued in a mocking, pretentious manner, his voice turning spiteful by the end.

It was cold outside, yet drops of sweat swelled on Rose's forehead. Gathering herself, trying to calm the chill running down her spine. "It's been a long time, Tapas. I thought you must have forgotten about me and moved on." Rose stammered, "I wanted to apologize but … It's all in the past now, … why…." she trailed off without finishing her sentence, clutching the receiver with both hands to steady its trembling, which matched the shaking in her legs.

"Do you know how long it took to find you?" Rose knew well that it wasn't a question, but rather an accusation. It was a statement meant to press guilt into her chest for the years she had eluded him.

"You left without a word. Do you know how upsetting it was... how embarrassing. If we were to part ways, don't you think you should have said so to me… on my face. Rather than running away in the middle of the night like a coward and a cheat."

Rose could feel her pulse rising. She knew he would be hurt, might get furious, and would look for her. But it had never occurred to her that her actions would cause him embarrassment, humiliation in front of his peers, his gang of men who bowed to him regardless of whether his actions were right or wrong. Everyone must have found out, and yes, he must have felt mortified, struggling to explain why she had managed to fool him and vanish into thin air. Tears rolled down the sides of her face as she cursed herself for failing to gather the strength to say anything more than stammering, "I… I…"

Tapas cut her short, "I'm coming for you, Rose." His voice darkened, deliberate, and chilling. He paused, letting the silence twist the knife before he continued. "I'll help you find peace for all the wrongs you've done."

She could feel his grin, smug, and cruel, as if it had slithered through the line to taunt her. Before she could gather her thoughts, the call ended with a hollow click, leaving her in suffocating silence.

Chapter 10

Imagine the confusion of an 8-year-old boy playing in the yard, suddenly hearing screams from inside the house. His parents had never fought before. He had rarely even seen them argue, and now they were turning the place upside down, screaming at each other. Little did he know, mere confusion was about to turn into a threat to everything he knew or understood about himself and his life.

"How did she find us? Where did she find the audacity to come and claim my child? He is my son! Tell her to go away before I burn her alive!" Tapas's mother was howling, her voice piercing the air as she yelled at the top of her lungs. His father, eyes brimming with tears, stood frozen, fury rising as he was accused of something he had done years ago, a decision he had made in desperation to protect his family. "But I was paid triple the amount I quoted, that ungrateful—" he muttered, trailing off with curses under his breath.

Tapas's parents were known as a quiet and peaceful couple. He rarely saw them sharing a glance or talking about anything other than their mundane responsibilities and obligations towards their son or family, but they were good to him. He was only five when he learned about his biological mother. Mira had passed away during childbirth, leaving the baby to be raised by her younger sister, Aun, who took on the role of his mother. Over the years, whispers echoed in the lobby or veranda about the woman who was gone, her love for Tapas's father, and his unwavering devotion to her.

Though Tapas was too young to understand fully, he occasionally caught fragments of conversations about Mira's struggles: multiple miscarriages caused by unknown medical issues, which had plunged her into deep depression. Yet, even in her darkest moments, her husband, Musaid, was her one constant source of hope, doing everything he could to bring a smile to her face.

Musaid Amin was a humble man. Coming from a mediocre background, after losing his wife to lack of appropriate medical help, especially during the miscarriages, and depression which followed and then losing her altogether to the complications, his simple village couldn't help. Musaid invested all his time and energy into building a safe environment, financially equipped to take care of his family and look after all their worldly needs. But even after years, what still haunted him, apart from not having his love alive and healthy beside him, was the lie he had told her on her deathbed.

During Mira's final pregnancy, just before Tapas came into their lives, Musaid was consumed with unease and dread. He prayed silently, tormented by the fear that Mira would once again have to endure the subtle ridicule of their family and villagers, the whispers, and judgment that had weighed heavily on her. By the ninth month, her despair was palpable, and his desperation pushed him to an extraordinary decision.

An unknown man, introduced through an old caretaker, had made him an offer both unsettling and prophetic: a healthy baby boy in exchange for a modest sum. The suggestion was bizarre and unnatural, yet it touched the deep fears that haunted Musaid. The man's knowing expression seemed to foretell the worst: their unborn child would not survive.

The terror of losing not only the baby but also his beloved wife gripped him. He knew she would not survive the heartbreak of another miscarriage, the shame, or the relentless despair of failing, once again, to bring a child into their lives. Tormented by this possibility, he spent days wrestling with his conscience.

A week before her due date, Musaid succumbed to the pressure and agreed to the arrangement. Yet, instead of the modest amount initially quoted, he gave up all his savings to the man, offering them a fragile promise of hope. He believed this baby could restore his wife's happiness and heal her spirit.

Before he could decide whether to tell her about his arrangement, tragedy struck. Mira fell gravely ill, and an emergency delivery was performed. Their child, born with the umbilical cord wrapped tightly around its neck, could not survive. Unaware of the miscarriage, his wife, even in her unconscious state, instinctively cradled her belly, her body, and soul mourning the loss she could feel but hadn't been told.

It was then that the man delivered the promised child at their doorstep. In desperation, Musaid rushed the baby to his wife, Mira's bedside, pleading for her to open her eyes and see the child. He begged her to believe that their baby was healthy and alive. Through her sobs, she stirred, opening her eyes just enough to glimpse the infant cooing before her. For a fleeting moment, joy, and peace lit up her face.

But before she could speak, she took one final breath, and her heart stopped beating. For Musaid, his entire world collapsed in that instant.

Under pressure from his family and bound by the lie which made his wife smile right before she left him forever, he married his late wife's sister. Together, they raised Tapas as their own, pretending he was their biological son. Yet for the father, the child symbolized his failure — a constant reminder of the day he lost his wife, the lie he told her on her deathbed, and the pain of not being able to mourn the death of his own child.

Thus began the journey of a father who, despite being perfect in his worldly duties, could never give his heart to the boy who saw him as his world.

Though Tapas was spoiled by his family, especially by Aun, his adoptive mother, who showered him with love and affection, he craved the attention of his father. For reasons unknown to him, his father remained distant, physically present but emotionally absent in every way that mattered.

Musaid understood that while Aun appeared furious on the outside, deep down, she was trembling with fear. The thought that this stranger could shatter her home, threaten the peace of her happy space, and endanger her beloved child's present and future filled her with dread. Her eyes reflected the terror of losing the one she loved more than even the god she worshipped.

Musaid took a deep breath, calming himself. There was no time to lose his grip on the situation. He gently asked Aun to take Tapas into the study, hoping the boy hadn't heard the commotion or begun to feel uneasy about the uproar outside.

Summoning his strength and rage, Tapas's father stepped forward to confront the woman waiting for him in the hall outside their home. The wide grin on her face momentarily took him aback, her head held high in apparent triumph.

"You're back, but without your wife, and my child? What happened? Did I cause a stir in your happy, peace-abiding home?" the woman asked sharply, her voice cutting through the air.

"What do you want from us?" Musaid asked, his voice calm but firm. "Let's cut to the chase. The man I assume to be your husband was abundantly compensated for the nameless baby he gave us of his own free will. That boy is no longer here. The child you're referring to now bears my name, my traits, and my upbringing. Tapas is my son."

Musaid's voice carried a fatherly conviction, each word laced with unwavering resolve, his protective instincts flaring even higher as he faced the intruder.

"He is my blood, my son. The man was merely the seed-giver, but it was I who bore him for nine months inside me. It took me years to trace you, but now that I have, I will stop at nothing to have my son beside me," the woman said with ease, though a trace of threat lingered in her eyes. "Paper cannot compensate for blood. The only thing that comes close to blood is blood in return," the woman said, narrowing her eyes, and looking straight at Musaid as if staring into his soul. "Since your blood will not quench my thirst, give me your soul, and I shall set your child free of his debt to his bearer and you, for cheating a mother."

Musaid had heard folktales of evil spirits roaming the human realm but had never believed them. Yet something in the woman's voice sent chills through him, and sweat ran down his spine as her piercing stare morphed into a sinister grin. Whoever this woman was, she was not human, he shuddered at the realization. Musaid's head suddenly grew heavy, his eyes blurred as a sharp fright found its ground deep in his gut. He had not only invited a battle, one where he might have to sacrifice his own soul to secure peace for his family, but he was to fight for his son's life, for the woman before him had come to collect the debt of their happiness.

"Leave, before I end up doing something I shall forever regret," Musaid said with folded hands but a stern voice.

"I shall return for what belongs to me," the woman replied with a cunning and sinister demeanour before turning her back to leave.

Days followed with an ominous silence. There was no sign of the woman, and Musaid and Aun, too, avoided speaking about what had happened, but they knew something was coming.

The air around them grew heavy. Their shoulders were weighed down by the chilling words the woman had left behind.

Tapas began to change in ways that baffled not only Aun and Musaid but everyone around them. They were certain he hadn't overheard a single word of the woman's conversation with Musaid, yet something within him seemed to have shifted.

Until then, it had never occurred to Musaid that Tapas wasn't his biological son or that he didn't belong with them. Even as he replayed every detail of his conversation with the woman, one truth remained unwavering: Tapas was their son, and no one could take him away.

But that certainty wavered when a servant brought Musaid to the backyard and showed him the butchered remains of a bird, precisely where Tapas had been playing for hours before retreating quietly to his room.

Musaid turned pale. Could Tapas truly be the blood of something evil?

And then it started happening every day.

The servants started quitting, and people became weary of going and visiting them.

It was on a moonless night that Tapas found himself alone in the forest. Though his heart ached hearing Aun howling for him and Musaid shouting his name, he had no control over himself. Like a puppet in the hands of someone cruel, he found his feet taking him away from his family, deeper into the darkness.

He had been feeling helpless for days now, longing to share his struggles but afraid of not being believed or understood. He felt accountable, even though his heart knew it wasn't truly him.

He had no control over his hands, which had been committing cruel and unkind acts on helpless animals and birds, pets who had been his friends since childhood.

And now, here he was, walking against his will towards a place even darker than the turmoil in his mind.

When his feet finally stopped, he was in front of an old, neglected cottage. A woman stood outside, holding a lantern, her shadow flickering against the dark backdrop.

"Where am I?" he murmured, his voice trembling.

"You are, where you belong, Tapas", the woman replied calmly, yet the air turned cold upon her words. "The man who dared to claim you as his son refused to pay for his actions. So, I had to take what belongs to me, be that be, what he cherishes the most."

"I want to go back to my mother", the boy stammered, tears welling in his eyes. "She must be terrified, not finding me in my room…I must go back, my mother must be looking for me", he said, breaking into desperate sobs.

"You are where you need to be", the woman said, her tone sharp as she stared into his frightened eyes, "and you stand before the one who owns you" She paused, a menacing smile spreading across her face. "I was the one who brought you into this world, and it is I you must serve. Nevertheless, imagine how big-hearted I am, that even against my will, I made an offer to the man you call your father, asking him to choose between his soul and you. He appeared to have chosen his soul… so I had to take away the other end of the bargain".

As the woman's grin widened, Tapas tried to stand, trembling so fiercely that he stumbled and fell to the ground. He couldn't fully comprehend what was happening, but the dense, suffocating air around him, and the woman's dark presence filled him with dread. Alarmed and terrified, he feared he had lost his family forever.

The woman motioned with her hands, and an invisible force pushed Tapas back, binding him as if with ropes. "You're not going anywhere," she said with an arched brow. "So, make yourself at home, my dear." She sat with poise on a large stone as if sitting on a throne, as though Tapas had invited her for a conversation. Chuckling to herself, she leaned forward.

"Let me start by saying it was not I who gave you away. My so-called husband saw you as an opportunity to fuel his hunger for money. Surprisingly, he found someone willing to compensate him not just with coins but with gold and cash, enough to fulfil all his vices and dark desires for years. That gave him the courage to go ahead with his decision." She paused, studying Tapas as if assessing whether he could grasp the weight of her words.

"He was a fool, though," she continued coldly, "for he couldn't hold himself back even after knowing I was called a witch by everyone in the village and beyond. He should have known that no lie could escape my eyes. Up until then, his affairs, and bad virtues were not my concern, for I, too, needed time, and space to empower myself, to engage in practices that required solitude. But the mere audacity of selling my child and lying to me about his death…" the woman scoffed. "He and his friends who helped him deserved the slow, painful deaths they endured in the months that followed. I had to ensure that no one dared deceive me again."

Though too young to fully understand her confessions, Tapas instinctively felt the viciousness in her tone. The coldness of her voice sent chills down his spine. Fear kept him silent, though questions buzzed in his mind. If she truly was his mother, why hadn't she come to rescue him immediately upon learning he was alive? Why wait so long, allowing him to accept Musaid and Aun as his parents and grow up in a loving home, only to shatter it later by taking him away?

The woman smiled, as if she could read his thoughts.

"Sacrifices have to be made," she said, her tone soft yet sharp. "You will learn with time that to achieve greatness, sacrifices are necessary. I wasn't powerful enough back then. I lacked the money and strength to fight the person who claimed you as his own. And yes..." she smiled apologetically, almost to herself, "I was in the middle of proving my devotion to my Master. You see, every student must show their dedication before their Master chooses to train them."

"I was alone, with no responsibilities to hold me back, and that made me precious to my Master. One thing led to another, and years passed as I pursued my zeal to become supreme. But then...my Master vanished. And I was left all alone." She laughed hollowly, a sound devoid of warmth. "And that's when it hit me: loneliness. It creeps in, no matter how powerful you become. That's when I realized...why not bring my son back? After all, you are mine to begin with."

It took five years for Tapas to finally be rescued from the cage where he was held captive by his blood mother. The years of struggle and repeated thrashing as punishment for his attempts to flee, to escape his mother's torments, changed the very foundation of who he was and the boy he was once growing to be. He had become a teenager who found peace in breaking things or causing harm to birds and animals. What his hands were once forced to do, just before being taken by his blood mother, was only a glimpse of what was to come.

The woman had instilled deep within him an obsession with hurting those he truly cared for, hoping it might free him from his longing to leave her and return home to his so-called family. When he saw his blood mother spare no effort in punishing him for disobedience, only to curse him later, pretend to feel guilty, and then blame him, Tapas began to internalize her words. She would tell him how much she loved him, yet how he kept hurting her by wanting to leave her for the people who, as she claimed, had separated them in the first place.

Over time, he started believing her warped perspective. Perhaps, he thought, this was how the world worked. Either you show power and take what you want, as his blood mother had done to get him back, or you break the will of the other person, leaving them with no choice but to stay by your side. Tapas, young as he was, had been forced to face both within a short span of time.

The first couple of months were the most difficult. Tapas tried everything, oscillating between compliance, and rebellion against the wishes of his captor. Days of obedience were followed by weeks of defiance, creating a vicious circle. The only constant was the outcome of each circle: giving the woman yet another excuse to punish the boy, fuelled by rage, seeing his desperation to escape and return to the life he had once known before her.

By the end of the year, even Tapas found it difficult to reason why he kept trying to leave or to hold onto the faint hope of ever escaping. He had come to realize that the woman, whom the hunters addressed as Rue, had no intention of ever letting him go.

The three hunters were the only ones who ever came to their door. They, too, would only show up when she summoned them, which again was a mystery for Tapas. They brought her all kinds of odd remains, what appeared to be animals, birds, and once even a liquid that looked like water but stank for days thereafter. Tapas gradually realized it was all for her rituals, which she preferred performing alone, locked inside the cottage.

Perhaps that was why he was forced to stay tied in the cage outside the cottage, he reasoned to himself.

Rue had told him it was because he had tried to escape too many times and needed to earn her trust to be granted a proper place to live. But the cage remained, and so did the rope tethered to his leg. Rue had "kindly" provided a small hole in one corner of the elaborate cage for him to relieve himself when she wasn't around. When she was home, Tapas was allowed the "privilege" of going into the forest for privacy—a fleeting moment of freedom that felt like a gift. Yet Rue made sure he never forgot his captivity, warning him of the invisible rope that was always tied to his neck.

Tapas had experienced its power early on, when he tried to run away. The rope would constrict mercilessly if he ventured anywhere beyond 20 feet from the cage. At times, he would sit at the very edge of its reach, staring into the forest, only to return when exhaustion and hunger forced him back. Food was scarce. Rue, a staunch hunter, rarely spared him scraps from her meals. If he couldn't find something edible for days, she tossed him leftovers. Other times, whatever meagre find he scavenged felt like a feast. Hunger, combined with relentless punishments for even the most minor rebellion, eventually crushed his will to escape. He resigned himself to his circumstances, forgetting the reasons for returning to civilisation.

Rue ensured his resolve stayed broken. She frequently mentioned how his so-called parents had found another child to take his place. "If they really cared, they would have found you by now," she scoffed now and then when he'd look hopeless, reminding him it had been three years since his disappearance. Tapas was too young to see through the lies or the maze of manipulation Rue had swung around him. Her patch of woods was shrouded in a magical haze, hiding them from the world. No one, except for the hunters carrying special bundles of bay leaves with enchanted spells, could see through the fog to find the cottage.

It was during this time that one of the hunters learned about the bounty placed on the mystical woman who had abducted the sole heir of the Amin family. The promised reward was substantial enough to compel him to appear before Musaid the very next morning.

Musaid gathered his men, and they listened attentively to every detail shared by the hunter, who had agreed to guide them to the cottage. The hunter had informed them that the dense fog surrounding the cottage would be easier to penetrate during a full moon, eliminating the need for the spellbound bay leaves usually required to pass through. This was one of the tips Rue herself had shared with the hunters in case they ever misplaced the magical leaves. Knowing the timing was perfect, Musaid wasted no time, and quickly assembled his men to prepare for the mission that night.

While rage boiled inside Musaid, fuelling his desire for vengeance against the person who had shattered the peace and happiness of his home, he was equally overwhelmed by the thought of finally being able to see his son again. Every negative emotion he had once harboured was gradually washed away by the passage of time, leaving only fragments of longing, longing for the child whose laughter and playfulness had once filled their home with happiness, peace, and prosperity.

As time went by, his need to find his son grew stronger, and so did his fury towards the woman who had taken him. Knowing she was known to be a witch only stoked his anger further. He understood how humans craved for power – for supremacy.

People find excuses to hurt one another or ruin homes just so the one less fortunate would be left with no option but to plead for mercy. But people who took shelter of magic to ruin families were far worse for him than the ones who used other means. For Musaid, the prayers, spells, and chants were only meant to seek blessings and shelter for those in need. To protect and cater to the ones less privileged. Learning about Rue and how she held Tapas in her captivity proved Musaid right on his firm belief that it wasn't her motherly instincts which made her take away another mother's child, but her greed for attaining everything she wished for.

The initial months after the disappearance were the most tormenting for the family. Their child had vanished into thin air, and no one could offer guidance or information about his whereabouts. Musaid left no stone unturned. He sought help from every possible source, making acquaintances from every sphere of society and even compensating foes for the slightest bit of news. Yet, all efforts were in vain. No one had seen even a glimpse of the child.

As years passed, others moved on, but not Musaid and Aun. For them, the world had stopped the very night their son was abducted, their lives thereafter consumed by the endless wait for his return. Lost and desperate, the only option left was to spread word of a bounty, hoping that one day, someone would come forward to help them. Much to his patience and determination, the day had finally arrived.

Finding the hunter at his door, Musaid's eyes swelled with tears, and his heart ached for the years spent waiting and praying for this very moment. However, hearing about the condition of his son, hungry, broken, and suffering, pierced Musaid's heart like a deep dagger, making it hard to breathe.

Unable to shake off the dread of facing Tapas, Musaid grappled with the pain his son must have endured, feeling wronged on so many levels. Having been failed by his parents, first in protecting him, and then in rescuing him from the clutches of the cruel woman whose eyes reeked of malice, weighed heavily on Musaid's heart. All he could do was promise himself that he would leave no stone unturned in bringing his son back to his home safe and sound.

It was a quick break-and-enter. The men checked the perimeter, but there was no trace of Rue in or around the cottage. Musaid didn't meet Tapas's eyes. With blurry vision, he untied the shackles on Tapas's ankle, checked the boy with his hands for any other chains or ropes, and finally reached his face. Holding his son's face in his hands, he looked into those empty eyes, and streams of tears fell freely.

"Where have I not looked for you? Why did you run away? Why did you leave us?" Musaid couldn't hold back the hurt ripping through him. He embraced Tapas in a warm, fatherly hug, tucking the boy's head against his chest. In that moment, he felt whole again.

Realizing they didn't have much time, one of the men, standing beside the hunter, and addressing concerns about what they should do if they encountered the witch on their way back, suggested they leave as quickly as possible. The rest of the discussion, he said, could happen once they were back in the safety of the village. He also suggested that it might appear as though the boy had run away on his own, and Rue might not waste time tracking the intruders.

Musaid noticed the hunter and his men, though doing their best to pretend they weren't afraid, couldn't hide the fear in their eyes. They were petrified of confronting the witch, knowing that, allegedly, they were taking away her "son." Musaid agreed that it was best to take Tapas home first. He looked at Tapas with pleading eyes, urging him to follow.

Tapas was as calm as the sea, his eyes vacant. He confided in Musaid that there was an invisible rope tied to his neck that tightened if he dared to go more than 20 feet from the cottage. Musaid believed him. From what he understood of Rue, he was sure she must have used magic to bind Tapas within the vicinity of this secluded corner.

"We'll deal with the rope once we reach 20 feet," Musaid assured him, his words sending a strange sensation down Tapas's spine. For the first time in years, someone was speaking directly to him, looking at him with concern. After so long, he could hear a voice filled with care. He couldn't believe he didn't cry. This was the moment his heart had prayed for every single night since he left home: for his father to come and rescue him.

Tapas stood up and took his father's outstretched hand. They kept walking in the dark, lanterns lighting their way. Ten feet turned to twenty, then thirty, and so on, but nothing appeared to stop them.

Within a couple of hours, the group re-entered familiar territory, and within another hour, they reached the Amin residence.

Chapter 11

Call it fate or call it circumstances, after everything the Amin family had gone through, Tapas's return was nothing less than a miracle for them. Rue never showed up, and Tapas never shared what his last conversation with her was like. She had never mentioned she was leaving him or, to put it correctly, letting him go—but something in her eyes that morning was not simply strange but conspiring. She had never left Tapas alone for an entire day, but that day, after telling him how fate always finds a way and that her realization of needing to bring her son back was also part of a bigger plan, she smiled to herself. She looked like his mother, Tapas thought to himself. He could see the resemblance.

They had the same vacant eyes and a thin line for a mouth, which made it nearly impossible to decipher whether someone was genuinely smiling or scheming a devious game. He often wondered, staring at his reflection in the water whenever she would take him by the lake to wash himself. He would look at his face and see her in return. It was a dreadful feeling to be associated with someone so ruthless as her, but he was bound by blood, the most inbuilt, and vital connection someone could ever have, making his own self-image hazy and unruly for him to come to terms with.

Although his parents were exactly as he remembered them, they felt warmer. Aun started sleeping beside Tapas, bathing him, and feeding him all by herself. For months, she didn't let any strangers near him. Only when Musaid comforted her and noticed his cheeks returning to their colour did she allow normalcy to take over. Musaid began spending time with his son, filling the gaps in his education from the years he had missed in school. Everything seemed to be returning to routine, except for Tapas's moods. He remained sullen.

For Tapas, a child who once had a beautiful childhood but became a victim of secretive adults, the world seemed fake, and pretentious. His biological parents, who both prioritized their own personal interests, first sold him for money and then captured him like a helpless lamb pleading for his life. The parents he believed to be his real guardians had hidden the truth from him. Sometimes he wondered: if they had told him earlier, would he have been more prepared when Rue appeared in front of him? Maybe he would have come out stronger. But then, perhaps, the childhood he cherished so deeply wouldn't have been the same.

He reasoned with himself, trying to understand his father's perspective in keeping such a monumental truth hidden. He wasn't oblivious to the trauma etched on Musaid and Aun's faces when they saw him in daylight the very next day after his return. He understood how harrowing it must have been for them as well. But it didn't change the fact that he had been the one at the receiving end. He had endured the beatings, the bruises, the pain of being lied to, manipulated, and starved—fighting merely to stay alive.

Tapas tried his best to comply, looking appreciatively towards his mother, Aun, who had gone above, and beyond for months to make him feel safe and comfortable at home. She never left his side, not even for a moment. At the same time, she never once asked, demanded, or even showed curiosity about what had transpired between Rue and him during the years he was held captive.

Years passed, and the only constant in Tapas's life was his nightmares. He could hear Rue laughing at the end of peaceful days. On darker days, when his reality felt like a storm cloud hovering over his present, her voice would hiss for attention. He tried to ignore it, pretend not to hear, but only he knew how tormenting it was to have her presence lodged in his mind, always, at all times.

She was there, judging him for his good deeds, smirking at the mistakes he made, whether intentional, or not. Yet, not once did Tapas share this side of his torment with Musaid or Aun. He decided they had endured enough pain. Now that he was old enough, these burdens were his to bear, the debt owed to the vicious blood mother who had borne him.

Chapter 12

Gathering her courage and embracing the self-belief that she was the chosen one, Rose decided to dedicate her time to meditation and practising the art of magic. Following the detailed steps Aura had recorded and narrated verbatim by Anant, she committed herself to mastering it. Rose had moved out of the Rays' residence, comforting them with assurances that her place had been reinstated and that it would be best for her to stay there until Tapas was apprehended. The police, who had promised to keep a close watch on the area, offered further reassurance.

It remained quiet for several days, and that silence was all Rose needed to awaken to a calmer self. She had resumed working from her office, where everything, people, places, was exactly as she remembered. But something within her had shifted. She saw things and people differently now. They appeared surrounded by colours, shadows of varying hues, and Rose had discovered the ability to read their energies. It felt natural to her, no longer surprising. She knew, deep within, that she was meant to be different. No longer did she force herself to blend into the crowd, yet she maintained a deliberate distance from undue attention.

Her demeanour, her walk, her talk had evolved. Her aura exuded a calmness that seemed to soothe everyone around her. People found themselves drawn to her energy, which eased their pain, be it mental, or physical. Rose herself remained unaffected by the pain she absorbed, whether consciously, or unconsciously, for she meditated regularly, drawing out her true self, the stronger, more dependable version of her being.

When a person realizes that there is no knight in shining armour to save them, that the strength to fight, survive, and live the life they dream of lies within them, they transform. They turn over a new leaf, one that is as fresh as it is powerful, capable of weathering any turmoil life may throw at them. Challenges will continue to arise, and their intensity may magnify, but these hardships are not without purpose. They prepare you for the world you asked for, the life you envisioned.

Sunshine grants its warmth only to those who endure the chill and stillness of the darkest nights. The fire of strength and self-belief ignites only when you shed the tears of helplessness. Actual growth occurs when you find yourself alone and it no longer haunts you when you accept that you are your own knight, the sole force capable of walking yourself out of the dark tunnel of self-doubt.

Everything lies within you. The solution to every problem, every ailment, is within reach of your soul. All you need to do is quiet your mind and prepare yourself to listen.

Having realized all this, what Rose didn't understand was why Tapas seemed to harbour such hatred toward her. She could comprehend the blow she must have dealt to his ego by vanishing from his life, but why had she been forced to endure such torment, pain, and ridicule before that... When all she ever did was care for him genuinely and tried to mould herself for his happiness and peace.

To clarify, Tapas didn't hate Rose; he never did. In truth, she really was special to him. But life had other plans, and Tapas couldn't help but become a mere puppet, bound by the weight of his debts.

It was a moonless night when Rose received the call. The unknown number blinking on her landline sent a shiver of cold through her. Somehow, she knew who it was, and no matter how prepared she thought she was for the confrontation, the anticipation still held the power to weaken her knees.

Rose turned to the mirror, her eyes meeting her reflection. She was no longer helpless, she told herself, and this time, she would not run—she would fight. Her resolve could be heard in her voice.

Rose prepared herself to leave. With Anant in one hand and her other hand in her jacket, she stood in front of the mirror. Looking onto her reflection, she started chanting spells for protection.

Anant, glowing white, warmed in Rose's embrace.

"Ask for peace of mind and soul, Rose. More than anything, my dear, darkness fears peace, and tranquillity. The darkness of an unrestful mind cannot shake a person who is at peace within. Know who you are, accept the beauty in your power, and stand upright to heal, not to fight."

Rose frowned upon hearing Anant requesting her to chant spells to strengthen her healing powers instead of asking her to be strong and put up a good fight.

"It is not about Tapas, Rose. What you are about to face is a test of your zeal to forgive, heal, and protect," Anant said reassuringly. "I believe in you, and I know, when the time comes, you'll understand what I mean."

Rose nodded in agreement. She comprehended well that, even when one doesn't completely understand a situation, one must trust the voice within. If Anant was asking her to bring peace to her state of mind and not allow it to revisit the past to ignite aggression within her, there must be a reason, and she must comply.

Tapas had asked Rose to come to the southern end of the town and take the straight road off the mountain. The road led down into the valley, through dark woods known to be the territory of wild boars. These woods were considered unsafe to traverse, and as a warning, people avoided installing streetlights along the track or anywhere nearby, marking it as a place of danger not to be entered. Rose understood well that this was exactly what Tapas must be counting on.

By the time Rose reached the entrance to the valley, it was already ten at night. It had taken her an hour-long walk from the town where her cab had dropped her off, refusing to go any further on the broken road. She didn't argue.

She kept walking in the dark, a torch in one hand and Anant in the other. She had decided to keep him close. She needed as much support from her inner self as from her sole supporter in this big, wide world. Even in the pitch-dark and silent valley, with no birds chirping, or cawing, she could hear the faint clanking of metal somewhere far off. She knew that's where she was supposed to go. Tapas had told her to come to the centre of the valley and assured her she would easily find her way because she was meant to be there. However, his words had sparked fear and uncertainty in her when she first heard them. But now, as she followed the sounds of pained, strained cries, and the grunts of men, she wasn't as petrified – she was somewhat hopeful to hold the same strength Aameen and Aara held, believing in their love, and will to protect one another.

She could hear overlapping chatter but couldn't quite make out what they were saying. They seemed preoccupied with something, something she needed to untangle to survive. This possibility didn't surprise her. She remembered Tapas being the incarnation of Bhariman and his vow to be born whenever she took the form of a human. She understood well that her safety was at risk, but whatever the danger might be, she had one unwavering purpose: to free Aameen, even if it cost her life. That was the ultimate trust she had placed in herself to fight for.

When life finds a purpose, and you seem to understand the true meaning of peace and contentment, acknowledging a sense of belonging to the world and the people around you, when you smile and others smile with you because they also feel safe around you, the world becomes a better place. You start enjoying life, living it as it's meant to be. Rose could see how the change within her brought change around her. The people seemed livelier, happier.

However, Rose also understood that being born means one must perish when the time comes. Death is an inevitability, and one cannot fight it; instead, it must be accepted to truly live and fulfil one's dreams. Yet, deep within, she had the sense that this wouldn't be the end of her. Even so, she told herself that whatever may come, even if this was the last moonlight she stood under, she would not leave her promise unfulfilled. She would find a way to bring peace to Aameen and reunite her soul sister with the love of her life.

Repeating these words to herself, with each step she took, a ray of hope glistened in her heart. Rose could feel the warmth of Mother Nature rising beneath her feet. She sensed her body embracing the powers within herself and the energies of the nature surrounding her. Rose reminded herself that she was a gifted soul, with heightened insight, and intuition strengthened by meditation and her regular practice of chanting spells.

With that knowledge and acceptance of her true nature and the purpose of her life, Rose began chanting gratitude spells. She expressed gratitude for the land beneath her feet, the air flowing in and out, the fire coursing through her veins, the water within her being, and the forest that enveloped her, gratitude for life itself, and for her acceptance of herself as a whole.

Aathya was back in town for the weekend when she decided to see Rose. She had heard from her former boss that Rose had started working from home most days, so after taking her address, she decided to surprise her with dinner. She was just across the street when she saw Rose leaving her home. She called out from behind her, but Rose looked so lost in her thoughts that she didn't hear her.

It was the haste and stressed look on her face that made Aathya call Mr. Ray again, asking if he knew where Rose was headed. She confided in him that Rose looked like she needed help. Ramanuj didn't take a minute to guess. He requested Aathya to take a cab and follow Rose, asking her to inform him as soon as the cab came to a halt.

Ramanuj coordinated with Mr. Begh, who confirmed that the last sighting of the two unruly men was also around the southern part of the town. They had allegedly loaded two big sacks into a car before vanishing. The men did the math and knew that's where they needed to be. With the exact location of where Rose's cab had stopped, the three of them decided to meet and not explore alone.

Although they requested Aathya to go home, she confessed that there was something she needed to share with Rose. Knowing the current situation, she decided to inform the men when she met them in person. Upon meeting, Aathya shared that, call it coincidence, or fate, her college was the same as Rose's. She didn't know Rose had gone there too, and it all came as a surprise to her only after she had shifted to the hostel.

Aathya told Ramanuj and Mr. Begh that one of the teachers had recognized Rose in a photo on her phone. The teacher had then told her about Rose and Tapas and the relationship they shared. What came as news was that, unlike other couples, this couple had entirely different faces and behaviours. Even after Rose vanished, though people guessed she must have escaped because Tapas seemed overbearing, they really couldn't confirm it.

Tapas was famous for his kindness as much as for his temper. Everyone knew the couple was an odd one, but they brought out the best in each other. Rose was a very timid, introverted, and shy girl, but with Tapas, she learned to laugh and be herself around others. As for Tapas, Rose had become a sanctuary. No matter how bad his temper got, Rose would calm him down. But he somehow always hid his kind acts from Rose. People assumed she knew, but the day Tapas signed an agreement with a nearby school to enrol all the children from Rose's village so they could study for free, Rose ran away that very night. Tapas was left standing alone on stage, embarrassed, as people laughed at him. People thereafter assumed how unfortunate it is that even the best of couples seldom know each other fully.

Knowing this, when Aathya asked her teacher if she knew what went wrong between them that made Rose run away without telling anyone, the teacher shared rumours of someone beating Rose in Tapas's presence. As off and wrong as it sounded, every such instance always led Tapas to go alone into the forest at night. His friends could hear him howling and crying, begging someone unseen to stop hurting Rose. He would plead for mercy from god knows who and spend days repenting for making Rose suffer, though he loved her wholeheartedly.

After Rose left, Tapas was often seen strolling alone, lost in his thoughts, or spotted talking to himself. He eventually became quiet. His aggression escalated to a new level, and his kindness disappeared. After college ended, Tapas didn't stay in touch with anyone. He told his closest friend that he was going to find Rose and that it was no longer in his hands what came next.

It was the last few days that concerned everyone around him. His eyes grew dark, and his face no longer showed warmth towards others' pain. Teachers and friends tried to find Rose or any means to contact her so they could warn her, but eventually, everyone gave up. They left the concern behind with a mumbled prayer, hoping the couple would find peace, wherever they might be.

Ramanuj listened to Aathya with his eyes closed, recalling the conversation he had with Mr. Bari, who had recently resumed work and couldn't stop talking about the boy from his home village who had gone missing right after setting the forest near and around his home ablaze. The Amins chose not to report the incident and instead paid money to cover it up—after all, it was their only son. Mr. Bari couldn't remember the boy's name, but the Amin family was well-known in their village and nearby areas for their kindness and philanthropic nature. Considering all the good deeds the family had done for the town over the years, no one said a word. With heads bowed, they began rehabilitating, and replenishing the forest.

The boy had seemingly left town, claiming he was searching for the girl who had caused him a troubled life. Compelled by some dark force, he told everyone he had to avenge his downfall, confessing that he had given up and could no longer hold back. Everyone searched for him everywhere, but he had been missing for almost a year. Even so, the villagers still spoke of the dark shadow that seemed to engulf him towards the end, as though it had consumed him entirely. It was almost like a mythical curse, the villagers said, how, when a dark shadow attaches itself to a soul, no matter what one does, it eventually consumes everything good.

The boy and his family had seen the worst of days, but even after the boy returned home, the "witch mother" never seemed to release her hold on him. She continued to haunt him. Mr. Bari confessed that though he doesn't know many details about the boy's past, but what he knows for sure is how even now, the people prayed for him to find peace and return home. As for his parents, they had stopped coming out of their house and stayed inside. His mother had been hallucinating and was occasionally spotted near the forest, searching for her son. His father, though he didn't speak of it, bore eyes filled with fear of something unholy and sadness for being unable to help his son, despite all he had done and was willing to do for him.

Ramanuj had already discussed all this with Mr. Begh, so he didn't go into much detail in front of Aathya. However, he understood well that there was something more profound and darker about Tapas and Rose's past and present that they weren't privy to. Aathya was asked to stay in Mr. Begh's car until the two men returned, hopefully, with Rose.

Chapter 13

Tapas's face came into the light, and a flicker of tears appeared in Rose's eyes. What had felt like an eternity ago suddenly seemed like yesterday. The memory of how she had first felt when she saw Tapas, his eyes looking at her, came rushing back.

Her gaze shifted to the two men digging a pit in front of the largest tree she had ever seen. The ancient ash tree. Rose gasped at the realization, her eyes wide open. Ignoring the men who were now staring at her, she walked towards them without a trace of fear.

"Go away, you two," Tapas commanded the boys, who were almost done with their task. The two exchanged smirks and elbowed each other as they retreated, the sacks rolled up under their arms.

"You look beautiful," Tapas said, a smile glistened on his lips. Suddenly, a sharp pain crossed his face, and he clutched his temple with his left hand, stumbling to the ground. "Hah, look what happens when I think my heart has a say," he muttered.

Though he quickly regained his posture, Rose didn't miss the glimpse of sadness in his eyes. She couldn't be mistaken, she told herself. He doesn't want to hurt me, her soul whispered. He's tied to his dues and debts.

Rose closed her eyes and, with her free hand, began tracing a spiral in the air before her.

"Show me the real reason I stand here. Show me how to untie Tapas from his burdens. Release him of his dues, for he is just a child, oblivious to the outcomes of his actions," Rose chanted, channelling the powers within her outward.

"Clear my sight and help me help him," she whispered, her energy forming a tangible presence before her closed eyes. But before she could see or do anything, Tapas thrust a forceful gush of air towards Rose. Caught off guard, Rose stumbled to the ground with eyes wide open.

How ignorant was she, she asked herself while looking at the tall, strong figure standing before her. How naive that she erred in not giving any heed to the fact that Tapas, too, was a magical being. Before jumping to help him, how could she overlook the fact that it was not helplessness in Tapas's eyes she saw, rather, the sadness of being alone through his struggles.

Head bowed, Rose heard Anant speaking to her in her mind.

"Even when your intentions are pure and your heart is in the right place, the eagerness to help the person before you can sometimes unintentionally make you blind to the true nature of someone else's struggles, but overlook the real need.

Instead of understanding what the other person might be seeking, we often feel compelled to advise, preach, or offer solutions based on what we think is right or how we believe their burden could be eased, assuming it will alleviate their pain. Forgetting the fundamental possibility that what if the other person isn't seeking guidance but simply compassion and empathy, a quiet acknowledgement of their struggles.

In our over-enthusiasm to help, without truly understanding the other person's perspective, we may unintentionally end up making them feel small or weak, as though they are incapable of resolving their own challenges. Although well-meaning, such actions can be hurtful.

One must remember that sometimes it's important to resist focusing on the vulnerability seen in another's eyes. It's equally vital to hold back and recognize that some struggles aren't meant to be solved with unsolicited advice but rather be met with genuine empathy.

This delicate balance—between attempting to resolve someone's troubles without their request and simply being present to offer them courage to fight their own battles, their own demons — is crucial for safeguarding one another's self-respect and dignity. Recognizing when to step back and honouring this fine line makes all the difference."

Rose nodded to Anant's words of wisdom echoing in her mind and regained her posture.

"I know you never wanted to hurt me, and I know you genuinely cared. But why do you now stand here with the intent to cause me pain when all I ever did was be there for you?" Rose asked, tears brimming in her eyes.

Wiping her tears with the back of her sleeve, Rose took a step closer to Tapas, moving away from the ash tree. A sudden chill in the air brushed against her spine, making her shiver.

Don't go near him, Anant's voice echoed in her mind, and she braced herself.

"Tapas, talk to me," Rose said, one foot still stepping forward, her arm outstretched as if pleading for him to come to her instead.

"Imagine how unfortunate I must be," Tapas began, his voice strained, "that the person who gave me solace is the same person I have to hurt to end the miseries I've endured my whole life. Imagine my dilemma—knowing that the only time the echo in my head will stop haunting me is when I cause pain to the one I fell for. The hurt and pain in your eyes were the only moments I could breathe easier.

"You can call me selfish because I chose to hurt you only because it hurt me less than the torment I was already living through. Day after day, it eased my throbbing pain, and I accepted it as my fate. But that's not what I wanted. I thought I would marry you, and maybe, eventually, the voice in my head would quieten, seeing my hurt when I saw you in pain. But neither the voice went away, nor did I get the chance to make you mine.

"The voice told me it would stop if I brought you here, to this ancient tree, and chanted some words. It said it would open my eyes once and for all. It promised that if you loved me as I did, you'd give up your life's course, and here, we would start anew. You'd leave your old self behind, and we'd build a life in sync. I don't know why I was meant to do so many ill deeds, but I know I gave in too early. That's all I'd learned; hurting others was the only way to ease my misery.

"My head was never my own, Rose. Would you have believed me if I'd told you before? No, you wouldn't. Neither would I. But I had no other option."

Tapas's voice wavered, his words a blend of fragmented thoughts and desperate emotions. Yet, amidst his rambling, Rose discerned the truth: he didn't know his soul was trapped by a promise he had made in a previous lifetime.

Sometimes hatred runs so deep that, with time, you forget the original reason for your bitterness. All that remains is the bitterness itself. Tapas wasn't inherently cruel, but the echoes of his past self-consumed him, forcing him to endure torments life after life as penance for his ill deeds. This cycle of suffering had hardened him, turning even his present life bitter.

Seeing him now, Rose realized he still had a chance—a choice to leave everything behind. With her mastery of magic, she could quieten the storm in his mind, granting him the clarity to hear his actual voice for the first time, untainted by his circumstances or the shadows of his past.

Karma is real, Rose thought to herself, but it can be cruel. Watching Tapas pay so heavily for his past deeds broke her heart. Even in this lifetime, he had been left alone, forced to learn cruelty and evil at an early age, as it seemed to be his only defence against the tormenting voices within.

Rose didn't know the full details of his past, but to heal him, she needed to understand it, to acknowledge his struggles so that, at the very least, he wouldn't feel alone anymore.

"I can help you, Tapas. But let me tell you one truth: the solution echoing in your mind isn't the right one. Give me a chance to untangle this for you," Rose said softly, taking another step towards him.

"No, you can't help me, Rose. Only I can. And this is it," Tapas replied, his voice steady, and his face expressionless. "My mother asks only one thing: that I give her this. She has promised she'll leave if I do."

As Tapas spoke, the cold determination in his eyes made Rose's face turn pale.

Tapas closed his eyes, and Rose could hear him mumbling ancient chants. Anant let out a pained moan, drawing Rose's attention to the ground where she had dropped her book when she fell.

Rose rushed to pick it up, brushing the soil off its cover. "What is happening, Anant?" she asked, her voice trembling. "What is he doing?" A shrieking noise was rising in her ears, like someone screaming from afar, running towards her.

"Darkness is coming, Rose. Brace yourself. Darkness will try to weaken your aura. It will stir bad memories and experiences, and it will challenge the patience and perseverance with which you have stayed true to yourself, even after going through the hardest of times.

Remember what you have learned about yourself; remember that it was all you. Even in the darkest of nights, you were never alone, and you will never be alone because you are magic, not the things around you. You survived and led a pure, humble life because you stood your ground and never gave in to the cruelty of the world around you. You made choices, and every one of those choices was for a better tomorrow, for yourself and for others. Your warmth reflects on you because that is how goodness works.

The darkness will want to make you feel alone and isolated. It will create hallucinations in your mind, trying to give you reasons to pull away from the people you believe you draw inspiration and inner strength from.

This is why you were asked to strengthen your capacity for forgiveness. While Tapas is trying to break you and, this time, make the evil win, you have to keep your core powerful enough to forgive him for everything he has done. Your past is the only thing keeping you from reaching your true potential. Like every hardship, it is important, as it shapes you for tomorrow. You are meant to fight this, accept what is, and ignite the fire that still lies dormant deep within you.

Understand the rage with which Tapas wants to bury everything that brings light to you. First, the things and values that bring and reinstate courage and self-belief in you, and then he aims to bury you alive to set an example for people like him, who believe that hardships can only be answered by giving in and letting evil thoughts and beliefs take over. Fight for yourself, but liberate the darkness that still holds you back. Do not let the evil win, knowing you can be bogged down and taken away from fulfilling your destiny."

Anant took a deep breath, as if losing his strength to carry on.

"Anant, I can't lose you. Tell me how to protect and save you. Why do you sound weak like this?" Rose couldn't hold her tears back, hearing Anant's pain, and feeling her own head throbbing from the shriek, now so loud that her eyes hurt from staying open.

"Rose, take a deep breath, and hold yourself upright. It is not me you should be worried about, for I shall forever live within you. The purpose of my life has been fulfilled, and I am happy and content with succeeding in the mission my creators bestowed upon me," Anant continued, his voice steady with reassurance. "What must be protected is you, your beautiful, giving heart, and the pure soul you carry. You were the one who remained in the world the last time and every lifetime before and thereafter. The essence of life, the energy of the Supreme Mother to uphold goodness, love, and compassion, the voice to protect and heal one another, it couldn't be erased, even when they killed Aara and Aameen in that lifetime. Aameen's love and Aara's sacrifice kept you alive.

I cannot hold back the rage that Tapas is swirling against you for much longer. You must remember, Rose. You must remember the sacrifices made by others to keep their love alive, never to give in, to keep holding on. That faith, that trust in oneself, and their fate, their destiny. Stand by yourself…" Anant's voice trailed off, quietening before he could finish his sentence, but Rose knew what he was going to say.

With tears brimming at the corners of her eyes and anger raging as she faced the thought of losing her most beloved, Rose fell to her knees. Anant thudded to the ground, and she couldn't hold back her painful, agonizing scream, pressing her hands tightly against her ears.

The scream was so powerful that it changed the course of the wind. Tapas stumbled and fell back, breaking his chain of chants.

Rose opened her eyes, red as a cursed moon. Her mind raced against time, throwing her into the memories of her life, replaying each painful moment like a relentless tide. She saw her childhood as dark and lonely. She saw her mother, tormented and isolated, and her untimely death. She relived losing her voice to the demands and obligations of others, bending her shoulders under their weight. She remembered the heartbreak of hurting the only family she had left, just to leave the village and pursue her studies, the disappointment, and condemnation on their faces as if she were a thankless and selfish being.

She recalled falling in love, only to be thrown into pits of darkness by the very person she trusted, over and over. She remembered years spent repenting her choices, her life, and her every day, where nobody cared if she lived or died. She had no family, no one to come home to, no one to ask if she was okay or care for her when she fell gravely ill. Her absent father—indifferent to whether she was alive or dead—was another weight on her soul.

Every memory and bad experience swirled in her head like a relentless whirlpool, toppling her to the ground under the crushing weight of her painful past.

In the midst of the tormenting vortex raging in her mind, it was not Tapas she saw before her eyes—it was herself.

"Stand tall," said the reflection, as Rose blinked to make it clearer, to reassure her senses that she wasn't hallucinating.

Rose could see herself in the reflection, but somehow it didn't seem like her. The Rose in the reflection was more certain, more confident, more worldly-wise, it seemed. She had been waiting to meet this side of herself, the one who was there with Aara. It was

Aara's Vaani. The woman, the reflection before her, wasn't much different from the Rose of today. The only distinct difference was that one was still scared to fully accept herself, while the other had embraced and nurtured every part of herself, beautifully falling in sync with Mother Nature.

"Only when you completely surrender will you conquer. The darkness can be devious, violent, and cruel, but it is nothing more than the amount of fear and self-doubt you pour into it. Only when you fully accept the fears and embrace your past, the hardships that have shaped you, will you finally be able to see through the self-doubt, and it too shall cease to exist…" The Rose in the reflection spoke provocatively to the Rose of the present, showing her the urgency of the moment.

Rose reminded herself that it was the voice of someone who knew the value of listening to oneself. Even with the pain rising in her gut, tears streaming, and her head throbbing with the torment of the past, she knew she had to overcome it. She had to try to accept it all and not stop, but keep walking through the dark tunnel her mind was thrust into.

The current of timelines swirling around and the rage building inside her somehow opened a portal before her. Over the past weeks, the self-belief she had been strengthening, her inner voice now stood before her. The reflection was not only enduring the unbearable weariness she felt physically but also embodying the life she had lived, yet it stood tall.

Inspired by her own hardships and dark days, greeting her demons with the resilient smile of a rebel who refused to fail herself, Rose gathered her strength. Though it took a couple of attempts, she was able to stand straight.

"You are who you are because of the pain and hardships you have endured. Like soft clay coming to its true form only after withstanding the blazing fire, your past has shaped you into someone who brings light wherever you go. Darkness will always be part of the light, but it shall always remain beneath it, signifying where strength lies. The power of being your own person, the power to look adversity and betrayal in the eye, that's what made you who you are today," the woman before Rose said with certainty.

Rose thought of Aara and Aameen, how, for love, Aameen had sacrificed himself to save Aara from a cruel fate, taking upon himself the curse of being separated from her for generations to come. Even then, the evil force couldn't destroy what Aara stood for, her values, her principles, her unconditional love. Aara never wavered from her Vaani, never doubted her path, and never failed to keep her chin high, no matter the trials she faced.

"With every attack on the tangible things that bring me peace," Rose told herself, "Tapas is trying to destroy Anant, to erase Aara's existence, and most importantly, to annihilate me from within. It's all to set an example, to prove that through life's hardships, anyone can turn away from goodness."

"You aren't that weak, my dear. Face him, face your past, conquer it, and claim what belongs to you," the Rose in the reflection said aloud, her voice firm and steady.

The present Rose drew on all her strength to navigate the whirlpool of her dark past that threatened to engulf her peace. "They want to rewrite the rules of life, a world ruled by the animalistic, where only the powerful and cunning survive. A place where selfishness prevails, and goodness is scorned. They aim to create a world where humanity forsakes love, compassion, and unity, turning bitter, cruel, and ugly. A world where survival is not about the fittest but the most brutal, cunning, and ruthless, leaving no place for humanity, no room for goodness."

The voice of her reflection resonated in Rose's mind, heavy and chilling. She realized what they wanted: to ignite her rage, to make her pour it onto Tapas, to make her succumb to darkness and become what they claimed humans inherently were.

But Rose wasn't ready to give in.

As Rose stretched her shoulders, as if shrugging away the weight of the pain and torments of her past, the air around her grew lighter. The wailing of her old self and the loud thumping of the ill words ever spoken to her seemed to fade away. The earth beneath her feet still trembled, a lingering reminder of the receding chaos, as she looked down at the ground below her. Stepping out of her shoes, removing her socks, and standing barefoot on the earth, Rose recited chants to bring peace to the world.

The coldness of the soil and the dew on the grass beneath her feet seemed to instil a bold stillness within her, giving her the confidence to stand tall and to know what is truly important. She is, as she always was, the most important.

Tapas looked at her with inquisitive eyes. "Oh, you think you've found your voice, little girl? That beloved book of yours, all the magic it held when even that couldn't survive the thunder of hatred... You think you can save yourself?" he asked mockingly.

Hearing Tapas refer to the magic the book held, all doubts in Rose's mind vanished. That was the reason for lighting the fire at my place, she confided to herself. He must have failed to find the book, and that's why he burned everything there, hoping the flames would destroy it when he couldn't.

Rose took a deep breath, and when she opened her eyes, it wasn't rage she felt towards Tapas, the man who had wronged her in so many ways, but pity for the boy who had chosen the wrong path to deal with the struggles he had faced in life.

"We both were wronged, Tapas. Our lives were never simple or comfortable. We were never *given the opportunity to tread* a steady path. But what we choose to do, or can still do, with our present will determine our future. Let go of the rage and choose to be wiser," Rose said with a confidence she didn't know she possessed.

She was no longer the same girl who had questioned her actions, but someone certain of who she was and what she stood for. Her life's purpose became clear, and Rose embraced it with open arms. She was meant to guide souls back onto their paths, to be there for those who had lost their way, and to bring peace and love to those who needed it most.

Rose understood that Tapas's mind was so clouded with hatred that he refused to listen or give himself a chance to face his inner self. The solution only reveals itself once you understand the root cause of the problem. Rose began chanting protection spells to uncover what had ensnared Tapas so deeply.

As the wind swirled around him, Tapas's aura turned dark red and blue. It was jealousy, self-loathing, and antipathy. The spells transformed into chains of his emotions, manifesting the clutches that had held him from within, making him cruel towards others. Now, these chains bound him to the ground.

Unable to move, Tapas glared at Rose with rage.

"It is not me, Tapas. I am not the one holding you back. These are the shackles of your own hatred and self-loathing. It's not others you seek to take revenge on but your own fate. You have to stop punishing yourself and set yourself free," Rose said aloud.

As Tapas's rage intensified, so did the grip of the restraints holding him in place. He groaned in pain as the bindings tightened around him.

Rose began to glow, though she didn't realize it. Seeing her soul liberated made Tapas angrier and more embittered. Tears ran down his face as he struggled to break free, but he couldn't. The rage burned him from within, and the ground beneath him began to quake, as if offering him one last chance to return to his original, innocent self, free of hatred, rage, and cruelty.

"Tapas, let go… I forgive you for what you did. I know you must have had your reasons. I don't need to know why you did what you did, but I want you to live. I want you to accept your past and step forward, leaving behind the shackles of the darkness you've endured. You can still free yourself and start anew. Just take a deep breath. One deep breath, Tapas. You're only one breath away from setting yourself free."

Rose looked into Tapas's eyes and folded her hands. She knew he wouldn't be able to hold on much longer. Rose began chanting prayers for his safekeeping, for forgiveness from the Supreme Mother for his sins, and for peace to finally be upon him.

As Tapas's vision cleared, shedding the tears of rage and pain that had resided in his heart for so long, the restraints seemed to loosen their grip. He came to the realization that Rose wasn't wrong when she said it was him, his ill will, and cruel thoughts that had bound him all along.

Tapas raised his hands before him and stared at the bloodstains that had suddenly appeared. Though they weren't visible earlier, he knew exactly where they came from and why he could see them now.

"Rose, you were my beam of peace. I fell for you at first sight and hoped I could finally be happy. I thought the past would leave me alone at last, and the haunting voices in my head would disappear because you were beside me. But little did I know that our meeting was orchestrated—all a part of a bigger plan.

"My devious and cruel mother's voice tormented me every time I came back after seeing you. It brought me to a point where I swore I'd do anything to make her go away. And then… it all unravelled. She told me I had to find the ancient ash tree, bring you there, and sacrifice you. She said it was my due—my purpose for being born.

"I fought as long as I could, but it was to no avail. I'd sleep with blood running from my eyes and pain so tormenting it felt like my bones were being crushed. The voices told me the only temporary relief was to inflict pain on you. At first, I cursed myself for doing it. But gradually, my pain began to subside as if it were being transferred to you. I became addicted to the relief, coming to you just to get another night of peaceful sleep.

"Another chain of wrongs I tied myself to—being in love and yet tormenting the love of my life… What a cursed life I've lived and still breathe."

Tapas stopped mumbling and looked at Rose. "End this. I'm tired. No one ever told me why these things happened to me or why I was turned into a demon from an ordinary boy. Why was I given a chance at a normal childhood, only for it to be ripped away? Why was I left with scars that brought nothing but pain and misery to everyone around me—especially the people who loved me most?" Tapas broke down, crying bitterly.

Though reluctant at first, Rose felt the courage within her urging her forward. *He needs you,* her soul told her.

Rose walked towards Tapas and placed her hands on his head. She began reciting a prayer, asking the Mother to clear his vision, answer his questions, and grant him the peace which the little boy inside him deserved.

Tapas closed his eyes and let her magic ease his aching head. As the pain receded and his thoughts cleared, his mind was transported to generations ago—like a film revealing everything that had transpired between Bhariman, Aara, and Aameen. He saw the countless lives lost, homes shattered, and the struggle between love and hatred continuing through time.

He understood that his tormented soul from a past life had refused to learn its lessons and had asked to be reborn. The deeds of his former life had cursed him to pay in this lifetime, bringing him to this very moment, to be given one final chance, a chance to seek forgiveness and pay penance for his past actions.

The wrong paths taken, the lack of strength to fight evil, and the choices made, all of it played before him, answering every question his soul had carried.

When the visions ended, Tapas was on his knees, his hands and forehead touching the ground. Crying, he pleaded to the Mother.

"She who holds Rose close, she who Rose calls her mother, please, be a mother to me too. Take me with you. I want to rest. I want to sleep on your lap. End this torment. Forgive me for my deeds and grant me the chance to finally have a mother who is truly mine. One who doesn't expect me to be something I'm not but accepts me as I am, shortcomings and all. I was a child who lost his way. Forgive me, Mother, and show me the way to you."

Tapas prayed with closed eyes.

Rose noticed his tears softening the soil beneath him. The grass swayed gently, clearing the area as if preparing to embrace him. Warmth began to spread through his veins, bringing peace from within.

For the second time in his life, first when he had fallen for Rose, Tapas felt at ease. He felt peace.

With a brilliant white glow forcing Rose to look away, Tapas was gone.

Rose understood that he had been forgiven and taken to rest in the same place as Aara. She didn't miss the smile on his face just before he vanished—the same smile that had once made her feel at home.

In that moment, Rose realized that Tapas had brought her closer to home—not a physical place but her heart and soul. She had found her true self and the purpose of her life.

Chapter 14

Rose saw flashes of light, glimpses of Ramanuj and Mr. Begh; they seemed to be looking for her. Rose apologized under her breath and chanted spells to bring fog onto their path, making them miss a turn.

She was yet to witness her promise being fulfilled, and she needed a little longer.

Rose looked at the towering ash tree, standing tall as a silent observer of the simple attributes of seeking and granting forgiveness in a world that can turn dark and cruel in the blink of an eye, yet able to save itself only through pure, unconditional love towards one another and, more importantly, for oneself.

Like opening its arms and releasing a deep breath, letting go of someone as pure as Aameen's soul after centuries, fireflies flew out of its trunk into the night sky, and Rose smiled, knowing the promise had been fulfilled. The soul of Aameen had been freed at last.

Rose, with folded hands, thanked the Mother for her grace and powers in abundance for showing the way to the ones lost and to those who sought shelter within her. The Mother, being a mother, always stood by her children through trials and triumphs.